PARTICULAR FRIENDSHIPS

Also by Martin Allen

RED SATURDAY

PARTICULAR
FRIENDSHIPS

MARTIN ALLEN

faber and faber
LONDON · BOSTON

First published in 1986 by
Faber and Faber Limited
3 Queen Square London WC1N 3AU

Phototypeset by Wilmaset Birkenhead Wirral
Printed in Great Britain by
Redwood Burn Ltd Trowbridge Wiltshire
All rights reserved

British Library Cataloguing in Publication Data

Allen, Martin
Particular friendships.
I. Title
822′.914   PR6051.L539/

ISBN 0–571–14537–X

Library of Congress Cataloging-in-Publication Data

Allen, Martin.
Particular friendships.
I. Title.
PR6051.L5394P3 1986   822′.914   86–12032
ISBN 0–571–14537–X (pbk.)

To Philomena McDonagh

CHARACTERS

JEVON   in his late forties
LORNA   around forty
GRANT   in his early thirties
CAROLINE   in her early twenties
ANNE   in her late twenties

The play is set chiefly in an office complex in a present-day London television centre. The action takes place over an eight-month period from September to May.

Particular Friendships was first performed at Hampstead Theatre on 17 October 1985. The cast was as follows:

JEVON	Philip Voss
LORNA	Caroline Blakiston
GRANT	John Price
CAROLINE	Caroline Bliss
ANNE	Celia Imrie

Director	Michael Attenborough
Designer	Sue Plummer
Lighting	Peter Mumford
Sound	Jake Bevan

ACT I

SCENE I

Lorna's office. Late September. Afternoon. JEVON, LORNA, GRANT *and* CAROLINE *are watching the end of a tape on which a male* INTERVIEWER *is talking to a young* WOMAN POLICE CONSTABLE.

INTERVIEWER: (*On tape*) So, Penny. Your first week over. How does it feel?

PC: (*On tape*) Well, in truth, it hasn't been as frightening as I thought it would be. But it's, erm, a relief to get it over with because I was a little bit nervous if I'm honest.

INTERVIEWER: (*On tape*) And the next thirty years? (*She pulls a face and smiles.*)

JEVON: Oh, lovely smile! Yes, I like that. (*He makes a note on his foolscap pad.*)

PC: (*On tape*) Seems ever such a long time when you say it like that, but hopefully, from hereon in . . . (*Continuing, under the following dialogue*) . . . I hope I'll learn from my colleagues and from my own experience to gradually become, erm, a competent policewoman doing a task which gives me job satisfaction and which is of benefit to the community as a whole.

JEVON: (*To* LORNA) First take, was it, that smile?

LORNA: First or second.

JEVON: Mm. (*Beat.*) Are they ties those police girls wear? Or cravats?

LORNA: Don't really look like either, do they?

JEVON: No. More a frilly sort of . . .

INTERVIEWER: (*On tape*) So a twelve-month training period ends with young Penny Richards becoming WPC Penny Richards . . . (*Continuing, under the following dialogue*) She now launches herself into a profession which in recent years has come under intense public scrutiny and criticism. Fully aware of this, and of the personal dangers involved in policing an increasingly violent society . . .

JEVON: (*To* LORNA) I know what I don't like about Nick. It's the red hair.

I

LORNA: Looks worse on screen, I agree.

JEVON: It's just struck me. There's something about red people.

LORNA: He's not too offensive.

JEVON: And they smell different, you know.

LORNA: Really? Unpleasant?

JEVON: Different.

INTERVIEWER: (*Continuing, on tape*) . . . she's nevertheless intent on becoming one of Britain's 9 million, women at work.

(*The tape finishes.*)

JEVON: That your lot?

(*All eyes on* JEVON.)

Mmm. Nice girl. Be interesting to see her again in a couple of years. See how her idealism holds up. How was she to work with?

LORNA: Biddable.

JEVON: (*Looking through his notes*) That was very frank what she said about her superiors.

LORNA: I find if you stay silent in the right places the camera has a kind of confessional effect.

JEVON: They need protecting from themselves sometimes though, these people. But yes . . . (*To* LORNA) Are you pleased?

LORNA: It's more or less how I saw it.

JEVON: No, I thought it was very good. It was instructive.

(*Pause.*)

LORNA: I tried to . . .

JEVON: (*Interrupting*) If I had anything to say at all about it . . . I'm just . . . How long did you say it's running at?

LORNA: Forty-three seventeen.

JEVON: Yes . . . I'm still wondering about the attention span for a programme of this kind.

GRANT: It is a forty-five-minute slot.

JEVON: I know, but it feels more like fifty-one or two in places. (*Looks through notes.*) What's happened to the police caravan?

LORNA: You said it didn't deliver.

JEVON: Did I? I thought I rather liked that, didn't I? Now

2

there's a sequence at thirty-one about an accident, which is new. No sound at the beginning.

GRANT: We took it off deliberately so you have dead silence inside the police car as it approaches. Just the blue flashing lights through the rain on the windscreen. Then as they open the doors, bring up the sound suddenly so it hits you how chaotic it all is.

JEVON: Yes, it was very effective. I just wonder . . . And I mean, watching it . . . The other thing is . . . Because if your series is called *Women at Work* . . .

GRANT: Well, it was her first accident. And the silence gives it an eerie effect. A bit like that scene in *Mean Streets* where Scorsese . . .

JEVON: (*Interrupting, to* LORNA) I think I rather liked the caravan. I think that's what I'm saying.

LORNA: (*Makes a note.*) I'll see if it can go back in.

JEVON: Could you have another dekko? It kind of plateaus out around that point. I know the cuts always bleed, but . . .

LORNA: It's not really a cut.

JEVON: It's not really a cut, quite. More of a fillet. It's not a . . . (*Laughs to himself suddenly.*) I liked the . . . (*Laughs again.*) Inside the caravan . . . But apart from that . . . I'd leave it as it is now. How's the next one shaping up?
(GRANT *goes to get something from his desk.*)

LORNA: I'm seeing a rough of the cartoonist in half an hour. And we're all set to go on *Ladies of the Street*.

JEVON: Ah! The street cleaners. I'm looking forward to that one. What about the councillor?

LORNA: The magistrate. She's next.

JEVON: (*Getting up*) Good, good. Nice mix. Well, keep me posted.

LORNA: And Grant has a little picture show for you.

JEVON: (*Looking at his watch*) Not more holiday snaps, Grant?

GRANT: No, no. It's something . . . (*Gives* JEVON *a photograph of a strikingly beautiful, affluent, middle-class woman in her forties.*) . . . quite different.

JEVON: I say! That's not Diana, is it?

GRANT: Slightly more successful than my wife, I'm afraid.

3

LORNA: (*To* JEVON) If you can believe that.

JEVON: (*Offering* GRANT *back the photo*) She's splendid, Grant. Well done!

LORNA: You've to guess who she is.

JEVON: Oh, have I? It's not an idea for a new quiz show, is it?

GRANT: Go on!

JEVON: Hmm. Could be a fashion designer, I suppose.

GRANT: No.

JEVON: Gossip columnist?

(GRANT *shakes his head.*)

LORNA: I said it was the first woman to have sex in space and I wasn't even warm.

JEVON: Difficult. What does Caroline think?

CAROLINE: I know.

JEVON: Hmm? That's a pretty little top you're wearing today, my love. Is it flannelette?

CAROLINE: It's Moroccan.

JEVON: Everyone's been on holiday. Feels like flannelette. It's not cheesecloth, is it?

CAROLINE: It's just a shirt. It's what peasant girls wear for washing in the river. You get them at the markets. I bought loads.

JEVON: Did you? Mmm. (*Returns to* GRANT.) No, well, she could be anything, couldn't she? Interior designer, health-food woman . . .

GRANT: No.

JEVON: Oh, I give in.

GRANT: She's the managing director of Kenny and Robertson.

JEVON: I was going to *say* advertising.

GRANT: Sixty thousand a year plus. House in Chelsea. Guest at the Royal Wedding. But all that was eighteen months ago. (*Getting another photo*) She now looks . . .

JEVON: Not another drug addict, Grant, please! I can't bear it!

GRANT: . . . like this.

(*He gives* JEVON *a second photograph of the same woman in a nun's habit.*)

JEVON: Good Lord!

GRANT: Sister Margaret. Order of the Sacred Redemption.

Twenty pounds a year pocket money. No personal belongings and no contacts outside the community.

JEVON: Where did you get the pictures?

GRANT: Business magazine Diana brings home. I thought I'd float it as a possible for the series. We'll need something for the winter now the dinner lady's fallen through.

JEVON: Well, it's worth floating all right. Worth floating. Isn't it Religious Affairs territory?

GRANT: They've no plans for anything like this.

JEVON: You couldn't get cameras inside a convent though, could you?

GRANT: If we approached them properly.

JEVON: But what are you thinking of? A show about her? About nuns in general?

GRANT: Well, the series is called *Women at Work* . . .

JEVON: Yes, convince me! Come on!

GRANT: Well, here's a woman who's opted out of a successful work situation . . .

JEVON: (*Interrupting*) You see, I think your problem would be finding a focus. It's a huge . . . It's a huge . . . And then there'd be all the . . . I don't know . . . What do you think, Lorna?

LORNA: It's got possibilities, I suppose.

JEVON: Extraordinary life, isn't it? What do they do all day?

GRANT: It depends on the order. You get teachers, nurses . . . She's spending two years as a contemplative before she makes a decision.

JEVON: I'd do some more contemplating myself if I were you, Grant. It all sounds a bit spiritual at the moment. In principle it could be quite promising, of course, but . . . Commit a few ideas to paper, will you?

GRANT: (*Getting another picture*) There's another picture of her with her parents . . .

JEVON: Damn! (*To* LORNA) I forgot to bring those papers in you asked me to sign. Are you dashing off?

LORNA: (*Unsure*) Well, not this minute . . .

JEVON: I'll run and get them. I wouldn't mind having a brief word with you actually, if you're not too pushed.

LORNA: Will it take long?

JEVON: Little chat *à deux*. I'm sure the delightful Caroline won't mind declaring before tea. No, give it another think, Grant. Take a turn round the park this weekend. It is Kensington you live, isn't it?

GRANT: (*Trying to show him a third photo*) Notting Hill.

JEVON: I must sprint, anyway. (*To* LORNA) I'll be right back.
(*Exit* JEVON. CAROLINE *gets her things ready to go.*)

LORNA: Who's a clever boy then?

GRANT: Do you think he liked it?

LORNA: He'll be taking holy orders after that little lot.

GRANT: Pity about that accident sequence.

LORNA: They have to cut something or they don't feel they're earning their money.

GRANT: The slightest deviation.

CAROLINE: Bye!

GRANT: Bye, Caroline! Have a good time!

LORNA: Bye, Caroline!
(*Exit* CAROLINE.)

GRANT: What's the point if we never let the veins stand out?

LORNA: When you're a producer, Grant, you'll have your own pension scheme to put at risk. Anyway, he's given you the amber light for *Climb Every Mountain*. I'd do some thinking about it.

GRANT: Do you think it's a good idea?

LORNA: 'S all right. Could be . . .

GRANT: Right, well . . . (*Getting his coat and a couple of files*) See you Monday.
(LORNA *smiles. Exit* GRANT. LORNA *gets her things together ready to go somewhere else in the building, then stands impatiently waiting, looking at her watch.*)

JEVON: (*Off*) Yes, have a good shoot, Richard! (*Beat.*) But not too good!
(*Enter* JEVON *with documents, smiling to himself.*)
Richard. Going off to Hamburg on that co-production.
(*Sees* LORNA *looking at her watch.*) Sorry, Lorna. I'm . . . I know you've got a lot on.

LORNA: It's just that I asked Billy specially to work late.

JEVON: How is it?

LORNA: I think he's done rather well.

JEVON: Is he growing a beard, or am I. . . ?

LORNA: It's the unkempt look, I'm afraid. He's shaving in the evenings so his stubble's the right length for the bar at lunchtime. I think he's got aspirations for Arts Features.

JEVON: Well, you have to make allowances. He does have that terrible stammer. At least you can make out what Grant's saying even if you don't always understand what he's driving at. That's an extraordinary idea, isn't it?

LORNA: The convent?

JEVON: (*Signing his documents*) Cutting yourself off like that.

LORNA: I don't know.

JEVON: And as for doing a show about them . . . I mean, I know it sounds a bit negative, but nuns!

LORNA: I think it could be rather interesting.

JEVON: And it's not exactly family viewing. It'd have to go out around midnight.

LORNA: It's more wholesome than prostitution.

JEVON: Oh, Lord, yes. Did you see it?

LORNA: I half watched it.

JEVON: What did you think?

LORNA: It's all been done before, hasn't it? Prostitution, unemployment – they're things of the past now.

JEVON: I thought it had moments.

LORNA: I know, but did you learn anything?

JEVON: I liked the man who wanted to pay by Access. What was it she said? 'You've given me one flexible friend tonight, dearie – I don't want another.'

LORNA: Melda! She'll be doing another show about Greenham Common next.

JEVON: (*Beat.*) You know, I often think this would be a wonderful job if it weren't for these bloody programmes we have to keep making.

LORNA: Some of us are glad of the distraction. (*Gives him another document.*) Sign that as well, will you?

JEVON: Look, I'm sorry about this weekend . . .

7

LORNA: Just there.

JEVON: (*Signing*) I didn't realize she'd invited Fanny and Keith to stay.

LORNA: It's all right. You get used to it after five years. I must be the only woman in London who gets that Monday morning feeling on a Friday afternoon.

JEVON: We could still go out tonight, Lorna. I could book our little table down at the tratt.

LORNA: Followed by a quick poke in the back of the Volvo.

JEVON: When the time's right, Lorna. I can't just walk out.

LORNA: You've been waiting for the right time since the night Carter tried springing the hostages from Tehran.

JEVON: It's a big upheaval, leaving someone.

LORNA: Jevon, I'm the wrong side of forty!

JEVON: I know!

LORNA: I want to know where the mess ends.

JEVON: Soon, Lorna. It'll end soon. (*Touching her*) I was thinking all through the screening how I'd like to slip my hand up that smart navy-blue skirt that always makes you look so formidable and imposing . . .

LORNA: Putting women on pedestals is how men avoid women's real feelings. It's a form of inadequacy.

JEVON: I see. (*Beat.*) I thought your women's group had folded?

LORNA: It's weekend after weekend. Going into one of Grant's convents might not be as crazy as it sounds.

JEVON: Dear Grant! These researchers do come up with some crackpot ideas sometimes.

LORNA: I don't think it's so crackpot. It'd be a good foil for the others. We've had too much about career women.

JEVON: I thought that was the point?

LORNA: Give it another dimension. In fact the more I think about it . . .

JEVON: You're not usually this keen on Grant's ideas.

LORNA: It could be just what the series has been needing.

JEVON: Well, I think it's all a bit weird. Nuns. I think it's all a bit spooky.

LORNA: I think we should go for it.

JEVON: Well, I can't stand in your way if it's what you really want. You know that. As long as you know how I feel. Certainly don't risk it if you're worried how you're going down in high places.

LORNA: Oh?

JEVON: I had lunch with Lyall yesterday. He seems quite keen on the work you're doing. He was asking me what I thought.

LORNA: And?

JEVON: I said yours was one of the more imaginative teams in my section. Ready to expand into fifty-five-minute slots rather sooner than most.

LORNA: You told him that?

JEVON: He's having a few people round for drinks next month. I wouldn't be surprised if you got an invitation. I thought perhaps we could have a bite to eat afterwards. There's a new Bolivian restaurant in Holland Park I've been meaning to try if you think you might fancy it.

LORNA: (*Beat.*) I think I'll wait for the invitation.

JEVON: But you see what we can do together, Lorna? As a team. The old team. How we can help each other?

LORNA: Then leave Anneke.

(JEVON *sighs and* LORNA *makes to go.*)

JEVON: Just a quick drink, Lorna. Later on.

LORNA: I'll be working late.

JEVON: Till when? I can wait.

(LORNA *looks at him.*)

I'll ring you. Just give me a time. Seven o'clock? Eight? I'll ring you at eight, shall I?

LORNA: I'm not sure where I'll be.

JEVON: Then I'll wait here. If you come, you come. I'll take the chance.

LORNA: Are you sure all this gambling's good for your health, Jevon?

JEVON: I want to make amends.

LORNA: You won't mind hanging around all evening then?

JEVON: I can catch up on my backlog of videos.

(LORNA *smiles slightly and exits.* JEVON *smiles to himself.*)

9

A week later. Early October. Morning. GRANT *is writing a letter. Enter* CAROLINE *in a casually sexy outfit, which* GRANT *quietly notices.*

CAROLINE: Hi.

GRANT: Morning. Good break?

CAROLINE: Quiet. Went home.

GRANT: Hunting, shooting, fishing?

CAROLINE: Well, as a matter of fact . . .

GRANT: You don't hunt!

CAROLINE: I'm not very good. Daddy's something on the committee. How about you?

GRANT: Went to Di's parents at the weekend.

CAROLINE: Fun?

GRANT: Yeah. Blanching sprouts for the freezer all afternoon with her 'ma'; golf club retirement dinner in the evening for her 'pa' – it was hilarious.

CAROLINE: (*Sees letter.*) Is that secret?

GRANT: Letter to Sister Margaret's community.

CAROLINE: Is that going ahead?

GRANT: It's been shuffled into the batting order, as Jevon would say.

CAROLINE: Who's going to direct?

GRANT: (*Smiles.*) Who knows? (*Beat.*) Hey! How was your film thing?

CAROLINE: Oh, it was good. There were half-a-dozen shorts besides the one Neville worked on. Goldcrest were there.

GRANT: Really?

CAROLINE: And is there a company called False Eye?

GRANT: (*Impressed*) Artificial Eye?

CAROLINE: Oh yes, that was it. I met someone who works for them.

(*Enter* LORNA.)

It was quite smart. They had a couple of photographers there, so . . .

LORNA: You're not going to be in 'Jennifer's Diary' again, are you, Caroline?

CAROLINE: I was only in once.

LORNA: (*Emptying a bag of plums into a bowl*) My dentist must keep recycling the old one – I'm sure I keep seeing you.

CAROLINE: They look nice.

LORNA: It's my breakfast.

CAROLINE: Yes, I didn't . . .

LORNA: (*Interrupting*) What is it about food? You can smoke a cigarette in public without having to share it with all and sundry, but bring out a tiny bar of chocolate or some fruit because you're fainting with hunger and just try eating without feeling guilty!

CAROLINE: I don't want one! I just thought they looked nice.

LORNA: (*Eating*) Well, they're not nice. They're tart. They look nicer than they are. (*To* GRANT) Did you get my message?

GRANT: I'm just finishing it.

LORNA: Be careful how you put things.

GRANT: (*Reads:*) 'Dear Reverend Mother, I am writing, etc., etc . . . hoping to make a programme showing the reality of the religious vocation . . . dispel some of the more popular stereotyped images society has . . . series renowned for its impartiality . . .' Few quotes from the press . . .

LORNA: (*Dialling the phone*) Sounds all right. Put something in about not upsetting their routine. 'Sensitivity to the rhythm of their day', kind of thing.

(GRANT *writes it down.*)

Caroline, darling, don't keep *moving* that Fittonia!

GRANT: (*To* CAROLINE) It spoils the effect. Bit of casual disorder shows we're all too busy being creative to keep the place tidy.

LORNA: Fittonias are very temperamental. They start to wilt if you keep . . . (*Into phone*) Oh, David? Lorna Brooks. Hi! How's Mr Miles? Oh did you? I must have been on a recce. We working girls . . . (*Laughs.*) David, I think I might have a goodie for you. I'm thinking of doing something on a career woman who became a nun. Would you? Mid-Feb hopefully. Pencil it in, anyway. I can't promise anything, but . . . What? (*Laughs.*) Darling! Certainly not! It's a lady's prerogative. You're not the only boy in my life, you know. (*Laughs.*) Anyway, I must go now, sweetheart. Duty calls. See you soon, David. Blessings! (*Puts phone down.*) Dear David! Outrageous as ever. He's quite a sweetie considering he's freelance.

(*Pause.*)

GRANT: I was rather hoping to have a stab at this one myself.

LORNA: Oh? What made you think that would be possible?

GRANT: We have been talking about my directing something at some stage. And it was my idea.

LORNA: A mite adventurous for your first time out, don't you think?

GRANT: I've directed before.

LORNA: Some years ago. Anyway, it was outside.

GRANT: I've got to start somewhere.

LORNA: We want a sure touch on this one. David usually gives me what I'm looking for. With a little prompting. I was having a look through this requisition you typed, by the way, Caroline.

CAROLINE: Oh, there it is!

LORNA: It was very nice. I still think it's better to do them in the style I showed you.

CAROLINE: I thought with this one being shorter . . .

LORNA: They're very particular in Servicing. They like things in the usual format.

GRANT: Never forget the project number is more important than the project in this place.

LORNA: Standardization has its own beauty.

CAROLINE: Shall I do it again?

LORNA: (*Giving it to* CAROLINE) Doesn't matter this time, but in future . . .

CAROLINE: (*Looking at it*) Oh, you've done it!

LORNA: Well, I was here till eleven last night, so . . .

CAROLINE: You should have let me . . .

LORNA: (*Interrupting*) I don't mind, Caroline. It's my job. (*Beat.*) I want you to give Camden Council a ring this morning as well. Ask them if they can give us one street cleaner who isn't in the women's movement. The schedule's tight enough without wasting time arguing about why all

12

the technicians are men. (*Beat, then to* GRANT) Anyway,
David's as qualified as anyone to do a piece on religious
communities.

GRANT: Poverty of ideas, chastity of imagination and complete
boot-licking obedience to his superiors. He's perfect.

LORNA: When you've got his track record, darling, we might
start taking your odd ideas a bit more seriously.

CAROLINE: My friend Jelly went to a convent. The nuns made
her eat soap. They did! If they found you using perfumed
soap instead of red carbolic they made you eat it.
(*Enter* ANNE, *unseen by the others.*)
She says they were foul. Especially if you were attractive.

LORNA: Good job you didn't have to go to one then, Caroline.
I'm sure they'd have given you absolute hell. Talking of
soap . . .

ANNE: (*Interrupting*) Is this Social Features?
(*They all turn round.*)

LORNA: Yes.

ANNE: I'm Anne Fielding.

LORNA: Anne. . . ?

ANNE: Fielding.

LORNA: And what can we do for you, love?

ANNE: I'm the new PA.

LORNA: Oh! Are you?

ANNE: Lorna Brooks?
(*The phone rings and* CAROLINE *answers it.*)

LORNA: (*As* CAROLINE *speaks into the phone*) Yes, that's right,
but I don't remember being told anything . . .
(*She looks in her diary.*)

CAROLINE: (*On phone*) Social Features? Yes, she is. One
moment. (*To* LORNA) It's for you.

LORNA: (*Glares at* CAROLINE.) Who is it?

CAROLINE: I didn't ask. It's a man.

LORNA: (*To* ANNE) Excuse me. (*Into phone*) Hello? Philip. . . ?
Oh, Philip! Hello! How are you? I've been meaning to ring.
Yes. Philip, what's happened since we last spoke is that a
number of our projects for next year have fallen through,
I'm afraid, and it's meant that some other perfectly good

ideas have had to fall by the wayside. Including your old age one, yes. So, much as I'd love to use it, I'm going to have to let you have it back. I'm sure you can find someone better than me to do it. Have you tried the other channels? Oh. And you're still minicabbing? Philip, I'm sure things will start happening for you soon. You just have to find a good producer and latch on to him. Then it'll all happen at once. You watch. Give me a shout when you have some good news, OK? Bye! (*Puts phone down, then to* ANNE) Sorry about that. (*To* CAROLINE) Try to get their names before saying I'm here.

CAROLINE: Sorry.

LORNA: Now, 'Anne', you say . . . (*Looks in diary.*) Are you sure it was today?

ANNE: (*Gives* LORNA *a letter.*) October the third.

LORNA: Oh, well, then. It must be right. No one ever tells me anything. Where have you come from?

ANNE: John Rice. The show about the navy's new ships.

LORNA: Ah yes, I know. He's got a lazy eye, hasn't he?

ANNE: There is something wrong with it, yes.

LORNA: Anne, I was just saying before you came in – there's no soap in the Ladies. You couldn't be an angel, could you. . . ?

ANNE: Sure.

LORNA: I know you've only just arrived.

ANNE: No trouble.

LORNA: You know where it is?

ANNE: Yes.

LORNA: We're a bit pushed this morning. And as I wasn't expecting you . . .

ANNE: It's OK.

(*Exit* ANNE.)

LORNA: Thank God for that! We start shooting in three weeks. I thought they'd forgotten us. (*To* GRANT) You might ring John Rice some time and get the word on her. I'm sure she's all right, but . . . After three preferably, when his tongue's loosened a bit.

GRANT: Who was that guy on the phone?

LORNA: Philip Holland? He's a hangover from that young directors' weekend I did at the NFT that time. They were all whingeing about how inaccessible we are so I gave a couple of them my card. Worst thing I ever did.

GRANT: You shouldn't raise people's hopes, you know. If he's a young guy trying to get his first break . . .

LORNA: We are not the Medicis, Grant! Doling out money to every Tom, Dick and Harry film-school graduate who thinks he's the new Rex Bloomstein. If they need anything at this stage it's a spot of rejection to sharpen them up a bit. And if you're so worried about how the Nun's Story's going to turn out, I suggest you put your efforts into researching it, not sniping at other people more experienced than yourself. You've got two months . . . (*Going*) I'm in the picture library if anyone wants me.
(*Exit* LORNA.)

GRANT: Look through the negatives while you're in there, Lorna. I'm sure you'll feel at home.

SCENE 3

Four weeks later. Late October. Morning. CAROLINE *is reading the* Daily Mail. *Enter* ANNE *in anorak, warm tracksuit, and burdened down with bags full of files, clipboard, camera, etc.*

CAROLINE: Hi, Anne.

ANNE: Minor emergency.

CAROLINE: Not another.

ANNE: (*At the typewriter*) Lorna wants a high angle from a church tower of them cleaning the street. Vicar wants something in writing to cover his insurance. Was there anything on her machine?

CAROLINE: Oh, I'll check. (*Rewinds tape on Lorna's telephone answering machine.*) Have you seen the *Mail*?

ANNE: Are we in?

CAROLINE: Yes. (*Reads.*) 'A tantalizing glimpse of modern-day police training, but what a pity, in a series about women, that we weren't taken deeper into the particular strains they face.'

15

ANNE: That it?

CAROLINE: Mm.

ANNE: At least it's not bitchy. (*Typing*) That woman – what's her name?

(*The messages play back.*)

WOMAN: (*On tape*) Lorna, it's Melda. Section meeting for Tuesday's been cancelled again, I'm afraid. I'll buzz you. Sorry!

CAROLINE: Everyone out having fun while I'm drudging here on my own.

ANNE: If you think hanging round on street corners in this weather is fun . . .

SECOND WOMAN: (*On tape*) Hello, Lorna! Long time, no see. Why don't you reply to my messages? Does that executive chair still squeak when you have sex in it? Lorna, why don't you do everyone a favour and just fuck off, you cow! (*The messages end.*)

ANNE: Is that it?

CAROLINE: (*Turning it off*) That was a juicy one.

ANNE: Who was it?

CAROLINE: Lorna's old PA. Gwen. They didn't quite see eye to eye.

ANNE: The one before me?

CAROLINE: Two before you. She rings her greetings in during the night sometimes. Brightens the day up.

ANNE: Does Lorna know?

CAROLINE: Doesn't seem to. (*Beat.*) She isn't the most popular person in the world round here. I don't know if . . .

ANNE: (*Interrupting*) Inevitable, isn't it, if you're in a position of authority?

CAROLINE: I keep asking her to send me on a Trainee PAs' course.

ANNE: How long have you been here?

CAROLINE: Ten months. I thought if I could get some location experience . . .

ANNE: Might help, yes. (*Looks at date.*) Oh, Halloween!

CAROLINE: I know. I'm going to two parties.

ANNE: (*Smiles.*) Do you go out a lot?

CAROLINE: Lot-ish.

ANNE: Are you going with Neville?

CAROLINE: He'll be there. (*Beat.*) He's not my boyfriend.

ANNE: Oh.

CAROLINE: He's just a friend. I haven't got a boyfriend. There's a whole group of us. We just hang round together. We're really close though. Have you got a man or anything?

ANNE: Not at the moment, no.

CAROLINE: I don't see the point. Do you?

(ANNE *smiles and shrugs.*)

There are always plenty of men around if you have to go somewhere special with one.

(*Enter* GRANT, *carrying books.*)

GRANT: Am I one of them though, Caroline?

CAROLINE: Oh, morning, Grant! How are the nuns?

GRANT: Progressing. Just got permission to film at Pendle Abbey.

CAROLINE: Sister Margaret's place?

GRANT: Booked us all in for a weekend recce just before Christmas. Should be fun. Get Lorna out of bed at half-five on Sunday morning. Kept a low profile on why we want to get in there of course. No point telling them we only want to talk to Sister Margaret. Not yet anyway.

CAROLINE: (*Looking at his books*) They look riveting.

GRANT: Don't go too close, Caroline! You might get converted. Although I'm sure you'd look very fetching in a habit. (*To* ANNE) How's the street cleaner shoot?

ANNE: OK.

GRANT: Lorna keeping them all in order?

(ANNE *smiles as she puts her letter in an envelope.*)

(*Picking up* Daily Mail) Were we damned with faint praise in here too?

ANNE: (*To* GRANT) Do you think it's right not to tell them we're only interested in Sister Margaret?

GRANT: How else do you get in?

ANNE: Deceiving them like that. . . ?

GRANT: That's not deceiving them. As long as we don't just do another wank-and-forget-it show once we're in there. That's the real sin.

(ANNE *gets her bags ready to go*.)
Have you got enough bags there, Anne?
ANNE: It's cos I'm using taxis. I have to carry everything around with me. Bit of a nuisance . . .
GRANT: Haven't they given you a car?
ANNE: PAs aren't allowed one.
GRANT: I know, but . . .
ANNE: Officially.
GRANT: Everybody wangles one somehow.
ANNE: Well, I did ask Lorna.
GRANT: I would give them so much shit . . .
ANNE: I must go. They're waiting for this.
GRANT: Yeah, see you, Anne.
CAROLINE: Bye, Anne.
    (*Exit* ANNE.)
GRANT: If there's one thing Lorna's good at it's giving people a hard time and quoting the rule book in her defence.
CAROLINE: That's what she's doing with my application. She says it's too soon, but other people get round it.
GRANT: Don't let Lorna get to you. (*Beat*.) You'll be OK. It's easy for women here. Come in as secretaries then transfer. That's why so many producers are women now. It's harder for men.
CAROLINE: How did you get in?
GRANT: I was head-hunted.
CAROLINE: Really?
GRANT: I'd directed a couple of things independently.
CAROLINE: I didn't know that.
GRANT: Oh, yeah. Did a thing on class. Got shown at the NFT. Mid-seventies. Just after I left Sussex. Got asked to come here as a researcher on the strength of it. Slight cash-flow problem after we got married till Diana got her business off the ground . . .
CAROLINE: What does she do exactly?
GRANT: Runs a market-research company. Got thirteen people working for her.
CAROLINE: Wow.
GRANT: While I'm still here . . . Not for long though.

CAROLINE: No?

GRANT: No way! Direct a few things here in the next couple of years, build up a reasonable c.v. then I'm off. I'm going anyway unless they let me direct something soon.

CAROLINE: Cream always rises though, doesn't it?

GRANT: More a case here of shit floating. Shit and safety. They're the two operative words in this place. Look at Anne.

CAROLINE: She's weird.

GRANT: She's compact; she's efficient; she's got no dangerous genius flashing off her to upset anyone. She's one of the grey intake of the nervous seventies who'll tebbit her way up through the shadows, and no one will notice till one day she's suddenly made head of a department somewhere.

CAROLINE: Do you think Lorna would take me more seriously if I wore dowdy clothes then?

GRANT: *Women at Work*! She should be doing something on one of these new-wave Tory women who are muscling their way into power on aggressive male assumptions. But what does she go for? Silly, whimsical rubbish with about as much danger as Jevon farting in the lift.

CAROLINE: She's doing your idea.

GRANT: Yes, but it's *how* she'll do it. You wait till that first production meeting. Whatever I put in my report she'll take it to the dentist's. The end product'll look like what I wrote but it won't have any bite.

CAROLINE: Why do you let her?

GRANT: I'm not going to. Not any more . . .

SCENE 4

Four weeks later. Late November. Evening. LORNA, GRANT, CAROLINE *and* ANNE *are having a buffet supper.*

LORNA: This is pleasant.

GRANT: It's leftovers from Saturday.

LORNA: Oh. Do thank Diana for me. It must have been a wonderful spread.

GRANT: Well, when you're entertaining an Australian food magnate who wants to launch Old English picnic hampers on to an unsuspecting British public . . .

LORNA: I'd have had you round to my place, only it's so poky . . .

CAROLINE: Oh, Lorna, I got through to David. He's still having problems in Glasgow.

GRANT: Did that heroin addict die?

CAROLINE: Got better, but they lost a week's filming. He'll be tied up with the editing a week longer at the other end now.

LORNA: Poor David. Waiting all that time and not even a body to show for it. Deaths always bring a shoot to life, I find.

GRANT: What do we do if he's not free?

LORNA: Who knows, Grant? You might have to direct if we get desperate. Diana seems keen on the idea.

GRANT: Oh?

LORNA: Come on, Anne! Drink your wine! Put some colour in your cheeks!

GRANT: I've got one or two ideas for structure if I can start the ball rolling.

LORNA: Yes, let's get it over with. David'll have to OK everything at some stage of course. (*Beat.*) Once I have.

(ANNE *gets a notepad out.*)

GRANT: All right. It seems to me that the hook of this particular programme is that these women have turned the concept of work completely on its head. Instead of work in a materialist, career sense, they've opted to work for God. So, for the opening sequence I thought we could have some shots of a top businesswoman's life-style – international conferences, famous parties and so on – then cut to this archive material I've found of a novice in a simple robe having all her hair cut off.

(LORNA *bites a carrot.*)

I thought then we could cut to a close-up of Sister Margaret looking straight into camera saying why she's doing it. Just one sentence. Two at the most. Then cut to the chapel at night with two sisters keeping a watch of prayer, and bring up some Gregorian chant in the background.

LORNA: We don't want it sounding like *Songs of Praise*.

GRANT: It won't sound like *Songs of Praise*.

LORNA: We don't want people thinking Harry Secombe's going to come sailing round the corner any minute.

CAROLINE: On one of those fold-up bikes nuns advertise.

LORNA: Oh yes, I've seen that! (*Beat.*) I don't think Grant's amused.

GRANT: I just think if we're going to make use of this evening . . .

LORNA: I can't resist it sometimes, Grant. You take it all so seriously. It's only a television programme.

GRANT: What do you suggest then?

LORNA: I think we ought to have . . . a little more of this brie.

GRANT: No, come on!

LORNA: Yes, be serious, Lorna! (*Beat.*) We've got to package it properly. I think perhaps a little bit of social relevance somewhere wouldn't come amiss.

GRANT: How would that work?

LORNA: Well, if we opened with some shots of, say, urban dereliction – heroin addicts in Toxteth or children throwing petrol bombs in Belfast or whatever – then cut to the peace and quiet of the convent, it'd give us our 'in'.

GRANT: To what?

LORNA: To showing that society might be in a mess, but as long as there are people like nuns prepared to escape from it all and go pray for us then there's still hope. (*Beat.*) I also want to look at the ordination of women somewhere.

GRANT: What's that got to do with it?

LORNA: It's the same subject. Women and religion. And it's topical.

CAROLINE: It said in *Cosmopolitan* they're going to start calling God 'She' instead of 'He' soon.

LORNA: There you are, you see. (*Beat.*) This cheese is really rather good. Is it Paxton and Whitfield's?

GRANT: It's Harrods'.

LORNA: Even so, it's very good. We should be drinking Blue Nun with it tonight of course, but never mind.

GRANT: I don't see the point of my being here.

LORNA: Oh, honestly, Grant! Look, what ordinary viewers are interested in is why nuns lock themselves away for ever without the things that make existence tolerable for most people. Like family life, or nice new clothes, or having Melda's programmes to look forward to.

CAROLINE: Or bonking.

LORNA: That's right. You can sneer, Grant . . .

GRANT: No, I agree. Sex is something we've got to look at.

LORNA: Well, how do they go on without it? Do they masturbate? Well? Do they? Do they write each other *billets-doux* on the backs of their hymn books? They must do something. It's not natural.

ANNE: Perhaps they fit racing saddles to their fold-up bikes and go for long rides.

LORNA: Exactly!

ANNE: Or beat each other with their girdles.

(LORNA *looks at* ANNE.)

They have knots in them after all. (*Beat.*) I'm sorry, but you've got it all wrong. It's nothing to do with being locked up and chanting plainsong and thinking about sex. It's not like that.

LORNA: Oh? What is it like then?

ANNE: Everyone looks at what they do without, never at what they do. You can't just describe what it's like. Some of them don't understand it properly, even after forty years. All they know is they're doing it for God.

LORNA: I think we were assuming He came into it somewhere.

ANNE: You read a few books for the facts and throw in some romantic or prejudiced notions and you think you've got it. You think it gives you the right to make statements about a mystery, a calling . . .

LORNA: (*To* GRANT) The PA seems to know more about this than the researcher.

ANNE: Well . . .

LORNA: Well what?

ANNE: Well, so would you if you'd done it.

(*Pause.*)

LORNA: If what?

22

ANNE: If you'd done it.

LORNA: Done it?

ANNE: Yes. I did it. (*Beat.*) Well, I tried it . . .
 (*Pause.*)

LORNA: I see. Well. Thank you for telling us, Anne. Good to be able to pool our resources at the earliest possible stage.

ANNE: It's not something you advertise. It was some years ago . . .

LORNA: But you thought you'd tell us now?

ANNE: I couldn't sit here any longer . . .

LORNA: Listening to our puerile remarks?

ANNE: If you like. We're supposed to be making a programme to get rid of that picture.

LORNA: Oh, for God's sake, Anne! Oh, sorry! I suppose that's blasphemy, is it?
 (CAROLINE *stifles a giggle.*)

ANNE: It's one reason I tend to keep quiet about it. You'll treat me like an oddball from now on. If you didn't already.

GRANT: Why offer to work with us if it's such a difficult area?

ANNE: I didn't offer.

LORNA: They forced you?

ANNE: There were three of us available. One girl had been asked for specially by another producer. The other . . . didn't want to do this one.

LORNA: Neither did you. Did God send you to enlighten us?
 (*Pause.*)

ANNE: (*To* LORNA) I came because the other girl refused to work with you.
 (*Pause.*)

LORNA: Ah. I see. How very noble of you, Anne. How very Christian.

SCENE 5

The next morning. Late November. CAROLINE *is sorting through some Christmas decorations. Enter* LORNA, *looking black, as the phone rings.*

23

LORNA: Tell them I'm in Sweden.

CAROLINE: (*Answering phone*) Social Features? Oh, hello! How are you? (*Writes down the name.*) I'm OK. How's it going? (*She holds up the name for* LORNA, *who looks away disdainfully*.)

Did you want Lorna? She's out of the office just at the moment, Philip. Can I get her to call you back? Sure. (*Writes.*) Oh you've found a producer!

(LORNA *looks up.*)

Oh, she's brilliant! Didn't she do that series on mental illness?

(LORNA *attracts* CAROLINE'*s attention.*)

Yes, I thought so. Oh, hang on, Philip. I think I can hear . . . Yes, it's Lorna. She's just come back. I'll put her on.

(LORNA *takes the call.*)

LORNA: (*Into phone*) Hello? Philip! Hello! Linsy Eldon! That's wonderful. You see what I told you! Oh, I'm so pleased. Yes. I can't chat now, Philip. I've just got here and I'm in a flat spin. But keep in touch, OK? And well done! Bye, Philip! Blessings!

(LORNA *puts the phone down pensively.*)

CAROLINE: She's one of the best producers around, isn't she?

LORNA: She's all right. (*Beat.*) I wonder if she saw the same treatment as me?

(CAROLINE *gets her bag and makes to leave.*)

There's no soap again.

(*Exit* CAROLINE. LORNA *picks up one of the decorations and throws it down scornfully. Enter* ANNE.)

Ah! The Christmas tree angel! Just what I was looking for.

(ANNE *sighs.*)

Careful! Count to ten if you think you're going to have another outburst. I don't want you upsetting yourself. Unless you like punishment of course. Some people see it as a gift from God, I know. Was St Anne a martyr?

ANNE: When you've stopped baiting me . . .

LORNA: I'm not baiting you. I'm trying to glean some insight into your superior understanding of the religious life. For the show. You're not going to be uncharitable and deny me that, are you?

ANNE: I told you about that PA last night because you pressed me. That's all.

LORNA: I'm glad you spoke out. I don't want anyone working here if they're not happy.

ANNE: I'm not unhappy.

LORNA: A quick phone call and we'll have you transferred in no time.

ANNE: I don't want to transfer.

LORNA: Pushing the charity act a bit far, isn't it?

ANNE: All I said was that someone else didn't want to work with you.

LORNA: And by implication . . .

ANNE: Your implication. It's you who's on the defensive. Not me.

LORNA: Ah, yes! The wisdom of the ex-nun. I was forgetting. Do interpret my behaviour.

ANNE: Look, I stayed in a convent for six months, five years ago. It was a mistake. People try all sorts of things before they find . . . It could have been social work or advertising . . . I'm an ordinary person trying to get on with my life like anybody else now. I don't want to keep being reminded of it.

LORNA: You did the reminding last night.

ANNE: Yes, and I wish I hadn't.

LORNA: Was it traumatic then?

ANNE: Yes it was, actually.

LORNA: Still a bit tender, are we?

ANNE: I feel pain, if that's what you mean.

LORNA: Other people don't, I suppose?

ANNE: (*Getting her bag and going*) Other people certainly give that impression.

LORNA: There's no soap again.

ANNE: Why do you hate yourself so much?

(*Exit* ANNE, *as* CAROLINE *comes back on.* LORNA *sits down and flicks through a magazine absent-mindedly.* CAROLINE *goes back to the decorations.*)

CAROLINE: (*Presently*) I was talking to Geraldine in the loo.

LORNA: Geraldine?

CAROLINE: Melda's PA. Geraldine Kish. She said she got on to a trainee course in her first year.

LORNA: Things have tightened up since her day.

CAROLINE: She said there'd be nothing to lose by applying for the one in March.

LORNA: Are you thinking of asking her for a reference then?

CAROLINE: How can I? I don't work for her.

LORNA: (*Throwing magazine into out-tray*) No, Caroline, you work for me. And when I think you're ready I'll be perfectly happy to sponsor you. I'm delighted to see you've learnt how to wither people at a hundred paces over the phone, but don't let it go to your head.

(CAROLINE *gets the magazine.*)

What are you doing with that?

CAROLINE: Haven't you finished with it?

LORNA: Leave it there, love. I may want to use it again.

(*Enter* JEVON.)

JEVON: Nice and cool in here. It's like Borneo down at my end of the corridor. Must think we're all busy growing Christmas roses. (*Sees Lorna's fruit bowl.*) And damsons! (*Takes one.*) We are seasonal. Are they Christmas damsons?

LORNA: They're my bloody plums.

JEVON: (*Eating*) Are you sure? They've a taste of Christmas.

LORNA: Pity we have to eat at all. Hours wasted every day when we could be working.

JEVON: You need a break every now and then. Recharge the batteries.

LORNA: I sometimes think they fitted me with quartz.

JEVON: Caroline, you couldn't be a poppet and go get me something lovely from the canteen?

CAROLINE: Tea?

JEVON: Sliver of milk, no sugar. No, on second thoughts I will have some sugar.

CAROLINE: Lorna?

(LORNA *shakes her head. Exit* CAROLINE.)

JEVON: Not every day you're given your own parking space on the forecourt.

LORNA: How did you manage that?

JEVON: Just fell from the sky this morning. I've had my name down long enough. Must have forgiven me at last for all those naughty satire shows I did in the early sixties.

LORNA: And those searching interviews with disgraced cabinet ministers that reduced them to tears.

JEVON: (*Winces*.) Salad days. What did I do before all that, I wonder?

LORNA: What have you done since?

JEVON: Not sure I wasn't born here sometimes when I think about it. (*Sees decorations*.) What are you doing for Christmas?

LORNA: Oh, I thought I'd have a few friends round for dinner this time.

JEVON: Sounds nice.

LORNA: Mulled wine, roast chestnuts, port, walk on the common . . . I'm going to Portsmouth like I always do. Where do you think I'm going?

JEVON: There'd be nothing to stop you having friends round.

LORNA: You know I don't have any friends, Jevon.

JEVON: They can't expect you to go home every year.

LORNA: I don't mind. Family Christmas should be quite nice. Gerald and Sophia will be there. Her charming offspring will no doubt ask yet again why Auntie Lorna still lives on her own. (*Beat*.) Did you know there are more suicides in the run-up to Christmas than at any other time? There should be injection centres where they put you to sleep for ten days till it's all over.

JEVON: You don't want to come away for a weekend then?

LORNA: At Christmas?

JEVON: Few days before. I was supposed to speak at a conference but I've wriggled my way out of it. Anneke still thinks I'm going. I thought I'd see how you were fixed.

LORNA: Have you got some Persil tickets to use up or something?

JEVON: I was thinking of taking the car down to Rye, actually. You're always saying how you'd like to go there.

LORNA: Which weekend?

JEVON: Fifteenth.

LORNA: Can't. I'm going to Pendle Abbey with the team.

JEVON: Oh, Lorna. You can change that, surely? You don't have to go.

LORNA: I do really. We're meeting the famous Sister Margaret. Can't you change?

JEVON: You know I can't.

LORNA: It'll have to wait then.

JEVON: I don't believe this. You're going to a bloody convent . . .

LORNA: When I could be in a Goldenrail hotel, waiting for you to get tipsy enough to stop worrying about cheating on Anneke and strip down to your boxer shorts and start groping me.

JEVON: Steady on!

LORNA: All that puffing and groaning and reaching for tissues and 'How was it for you?' . . . We're getting a bit long in the tooth for all that, don't you think?

JEVON: Speak for yourself!

LORNA: Anyway, I've got to go now. I've found I've got an ex-nun working for me.

JEVON: Not Caroline?

LORNA: No. Not Grant either.

JEVON: Do you know, I thought there was something odd about that girl.

LORNA: Well, now you know.

JEVON: We'll get her transferred.

LORNA: She doesn't want transferring.

JEVON: Doesn't she indeed? I don't like the feel of this. You'd better tell me what's been happening, Lorna. I don't want any more Gwens in this section.

LORNA: Nothing's been happening. We only found out last night.

JEVON: All the better to act promptly. Might be best to draw stumps on this one now before we get into even deeper water.

LORNA: She thinks I ought to join up for a few months to see what it's like. Might be a good investment. I'm only a few years off my mid-life crisis after all.

(JEVON *stares at her.*)

28

I'm not dropping everything because you have a free
weekend for the first time in six months.

JEVON: I don't expect you to.

LORNA: That's all right then. Isn't it?
(*Enter* CAROLINE *with tea.*)

JEVON: Ah, thank you, my love. I hear you're going on a jaunt
to a nunnery?

CAROLINE: Are you joining us?

JEVON: I'm going to be a bit tied up that weekend
unfortunately. I'm sure I can rely on you to give me a
detailed report of what happens though, can I, Caroline?
My love?

SCENE 6

Convent guests' bedroom. Two and a half weeks later.
Mid-December. Evening. Simply furnished, to include a table,
chairs and two single beds. LORNA, GRANT *and* CAROLINE,
looking dejected and drinking Scotch, with four trays of half-eaten
food, and LORNA *holding a letter.*

CAROLINE: Spam fritters . . .

GRANT: Bloody hell! What can we do in forty minutes? Just
have to set everything up ready for her and do it all in one
take I suppose.

LORNA: It's the arrogance that gets me! (*Reads from note:*)
'Having given the matter great thought and much prayer, I
feel I will be able to give one day over to your project. You
will be here in Lent, however, when we are allowed only
forty minutes recreation time each day, and as my
conscience dictates that work and prayer should not be
interrupted by such diversions as light entertainment, I am
afraid that forty minutes is all I can offer you.' Light
entertainment!

GRANT: Been watching our shows obviously.

LORNA: Bloody woman! It's Anne's fault. They can tell she's a
failed nun.

CAROLINE: Where does she keep going?

29

LORNA: It's that cardigan she wears. It's a demob uniform for failed nuns.

CAROLINE: Where is she?

LORNA: In the loo. Passing holy water.

GRANT: Lorna!

LORNA: Oh, give me some more Scotch, Caroline! Help me think.

(CAROLINE *gives her more Scotch.*)

'My conscience dictates'! What does she want – the BAFTA award for humility?

GRANT: At least she's doing it! She's suspicious, and who can blame her? She knows what TV people are like. She's probably worried we're just going to titillate the audience at her expense. Drown her in all those clichés Anne got so angry about.

LORNA: Darling! You're talking about the British television documentary! Respected throughout the world!

GRANT: Yes. And I'm also talking about a woman who used to eat people like us for breakfast. It's *us* who ought to be showing a bit of humility. She knows what kind of programme we're going to make. For God's sake, she got to the top of the tree we're all still busy climbing. But she gave it up. For this. Deeply threatening when you think about it. But will our programme look at that? It won't actually take the piss out of her. It'll say she's rather noble and brave. But at the same time it'll be gently mocking. And we'll draw the sting. We'll anaesthetize, till what we're left with is a nice, voyeuristic look at an interesting oddity.

(*Enter* ANNE.)

It's no wonder she doesn't trust us. If we can use that forty minutes with her in the right way, she might just agree to do some more.

(*Pause.*)

LORNA: Have you finished?

GRANT: Yes.

LORNA: Right, you listen to me. You are not a producer.

GRANT: I'd noticed.

LORNA: When you're the one putting your name to things;

30

when your career and reputation are on the line – I think you'll
find it's a slightly different ball game. You might find you
switch your allegiance from these heroes of yours like Sister
Margaret who upset months of planning at a flick, to the
people you're supposed to be working with. Because there *are*
people in this business with integrity and vision, and they *are*
struggling – damn hard – to get things they believe in on to the
screens. It's not easy in a big institution.

GRANT: Doesn't mean you have to compromise.

LORNA: Oh, doesn't it? So what do you do? Do you upset the very
people who're in a position to give you more power to make
bigger and better programmes?

GRANT: I don't know. Perhaps we should all be mavericks.

LORNA: You'll never make a career that way.

(*Pause.*)

CAROLINE: The acoustics in that chapel are wonderful.

LORNA: Aren't they?

CAROLINE: (*To* ANNE) Did you used to sing in a squeaky voice like
they were doing?

ANNE: I sang soprano, yes.

CAROLINE: Why don't they sing in a normal voice?

ANNE: I don't know, Caroline. Why don't you ask them?

CAROLINE: You're the expert.

ANNE: Why do you wear black?

CAROLINE: I like black.

ANNE: You wear black because it's the fashion.

CAROLINE: I bloody don't!

LORNA: Caroline!

ANNE: All I'm saying is I did it because everyone else did, but at
least I'm not kidding myself.

CAROLINE: I only asked!

LORNA: Girls! Remember where you are!

(*Pause.*)

We must be mad! Coming to a convent on a Saturday night.
It's only quarter-past eight, Grant! What are we going to do?

GRANT: Trivial Pursuit?

LORNA: You'd better have the car ready for a dawn getaway in case
I get panicky.

CAROLINE: (*Looking at watch*) I'd better be making my getaway in a minute, actually.

LORNA: (*To* GRANT) *Why* did you only book three beds?

GRANT: I told you – I booked three *rooms*. A double and two singles. They turned it into three *beds* somewhere.

LORNA: I thought nuns were supposed to be reliable? Oh, sleep on the floor, Caroline. In here.

CAROLINE: I can't sleep on the floor.

LORNA: You can't leave me.

ANNE: I'll go back if you like.

LORNA: Oh, would. . . ?

CAROLINE: I've got to go now. I rang Neville. We're all going to a party and they need me to get them in.

LORNA: How are you getting back?

CAROLINE: Grant's running me to the station.

GRANT: I'll go get my keys.

(*Exit* GRANT. CAROLINE *gets her things together, including a copy of* The Times. LORNA *looks at* ANNE.)

ANNE: I don't mind going back.

CAROLINE: But I've got to go now.

LORNA: What if we get trapped? What if there's a fire and we can't get out?

CAROLINE: God's not going to set fire to nuns.

LORNA: When did you say the next PAs' course was?

CAROLINE: (*Beat.*) I'll have to go, Lorna. Jelly and Neville will be waiting for me.

LORNA: Ring them.

CAROLINE: They'll have left by now. Anyway, you're the producer. You've got to stay.

ANNE: Mother Agnes is expecting us at eleven in the morning. We've still got to finalize everything.

LORNA: What am I going to do?

CAROLINE: It's only for a night. Ring me tomorrow.

(*Enter* GRANT.)

GRANT: (*To* CAROLINE) Ready?

(CAROLINE *nods a polite farewell to* ANNE *then looks at* LORNA.)

CAROLINE: I'm sorry.

GRANT: (*To* LORNA) Remember – don't play radios or run any
    bathwater after ten.
    (*Exit* GRANT *and* CAROLINE. *Pause.*)
ANNE: I won't be needing the bathroom.
    (LORNA *gets her bag and exits.* ANNE *hurriedly gets ready for bed.*
    Enter LORNA *in her nightie.*)
LORNA: May as well finish my crossword. (*Searches.*) Have you
    seen my *Times*?
ANNE: (*Getting into bed*) No.
LORNA: (*After searching a little more and realizing*) Bloody Caroline!
    (*Stripped of this last defence* LORNA *now realizes with some alarm*
    that she has to spend the night alone with ANNE. *She looks at her*
    watch, reluctantly gets into bed, turns out the light and settles
    down. Pause. A bell chimes the half-hour.)
    Oh, shit! Is that going to go on all night?
ANNE: Don't know.
LORNA: It is. I know it is. (*Sighs.*) I can never get to sleep before
    half-one anyway. I don't know why I'm in bed. The pubs are
    still open for God's sake! We could be playing radios or
    running bathwater.
ANNE: They usually put a good play on the radio on Saturday
    nights.
LORNA: I knew I should have brought my duvet. I thought
    blankets went out with polio. Did you try the window?
ANNE: It's stuck.
LORNA: We're not locked in, are we?
ANNE: The door opens.
LORNA: I can't sleep without air. And it's too hot. I like it warmish
    when I go to bed, cool while I sleep and warm again when I
    wake up.
ANNE: Shall I open the door?
LORNA: I don't want the smell of that floor polish to come in.
    (*Pause.*)
ANNE: It's a shame about Sister Margaret.
LORNA: Grant'll have to get round that one. It was his idea.
ANNE: Are you going to let him direct it?
LORNA: We're seeing that Mother Agnes woman at eleven then
    we're off.

ANNE: Suits me.

LORNA: The hell out of here! (*Beat.*) What do you mean – it suits you?

ANNE: It does.

LORNA: Well, I'm sure we could both think of nicer ways to spend Saturday night.

ANNE: It's the place I'm talking about. Not you. (*Beat.*) I thought I was going to be sick earlier.

LORNA: You should have tried putting your finger down your throat and getting it over with. The rest of us might have been able to get into the loo then.

(*Pause.*)

(*Suddenly alarmed*) You don't feel sick now, do you?

ANNE: Don't worry. I'll go out if I have to throw up. I wouldn't dream of embarrassing you.

LORNA: I thought convents were your territory?

ANNE: You do a lot of other people's thinking for them.

LORNA: You have to in my job.

ANNE: You should try listening for a change.

LORNA: To other people's problems, yes, I know. Some of those scars take ever such a long time to heal, don't they?

ANNE: Oh, go to hell!

(*Pause.* LORNA *puts on the light, gets up and gets a drink.*)

LORNA: Is it like the place you went to then?

ANNE: They had more flagellation where I was. (*Pause.*) It was horrendous.

LORNA: How?

ANNE: Everything. Up at half-five every morning; two and a half hours' prayer before breakfast; then an endless round of work, chapel and rotten food. All day, every day. No free time to speak of . . .

LORNA: Sounds like a trainee producers' weekend.

ANNE: You weren't allowed to talk to anyone except Sunday afternoons.

LORNA: What?

ANNE: You could talk about work. Or prayer! I was in a strict order though. They discouraged particular friendships.

LORNA: Which?

ANNE: It's an expression they used. Two sisters making friends. Getting close to each other.

LORNA: Worried you'd all turn into raving lesbians?

ANNE: Worried you'd make another person more important than the community. There *was* a fear of sex behind it somewhere, but . . . It was more to do with being distracted from God. They split you up if they saw it happening.

LORNA: No wonder candle firms stay in business!

ANNE: Men's jokes. Worried that women can choose a life where they're not needed. Ones who've been used to sex find it difficult. It's the closeness you miss. Knowing you'll always be alone.

LORNA: How on earth did you get into it?

ANNE: Sometimes wonder. Friend from college went over there one day to have tea and I went along for the ride. That was . . . Oh, it's all in the past now.

LORNA: (*Beat.*) What happened?
(*Pause.*)

ANNE: It was just after New Year. Funny. It was only a few miles from where I lived and I'd never been up there. We went into this reception hall. There was a big wooden staircase and a Christmas tree with lights. A sister came over to meet us . . . And that was it. It was like I'd come home.

LORNA: Were you religious?

ANNE: Not really. No more than anybody else. I had the same feeling when we got here today though. Coming home. But all the unhappiness too. As if nothing had changed.

LORNA: Sounds a bit Mills and Boon: 'I got there and it felt like home.'

ANNE: That's how it was. (*Beat.*) And three years later I was in. Ready for an idyllic life of prayer and closeness to God. Convinced it was what He wanted.

LORNA: I'd have gone to see a shrink first. Bad enough spending a night here.

ANNE: I was doing a wonderful line in the importance of humility – how it'd count more at death than being a society beauty or another Mozart. As if I had a chance of being either!

LORNA: Why didn't it work then? Or didn't the holy ones say?

ANNE: They just said it wasn't right yet.

LORNA: Helpful! Sounds like Jevon at a screening.

ANNE: I don't know why it didn't work. I didn't want to stay. I didn't want to leave though, either. Didn't want to fail. I hated it. Yet I can still see the attraction today. (*Half-tearful*) It was five years ago. I don't understand. (*Pause.*)

LORNA: It's only the attraction of escape.

ANNE: There's no escape from yourself in a place like this. It's the last place to come if you want that.
(*The bell chimes the three-quarter hour.*)

LORNA: That girl in the white veil.

ANNE: The novice.

LORNA: She's rather beautiful. Strange. I wonder how she's feeling?

ANNE: Can't be feeling too bad or she wouldn't have got this far.
(LORNA *looks at* ANNE.)

LORNA: You know quite a lot about it, don't you?

ANNE: I ought to.
(*Pause, as* LORNA *goes on looking at* ANNE.)
What?

LORNA: Nothing.

SCENE 7

Lorna's office. A few days later. Mid-December. Night. The office is in darkness. Sounds off of an office party.

LORNA: (*Off*) Come on!

ANNE: (*Off*) Where are you going?
(*Enter* LORNA *and* ANNE, *slightly tipsy, wearing party hats and carrying drinks.* LORNA *puts the lights on and we see a video camera linked to a television monitor and VTR set up ready to record.*)

36

What are you doing? What's going on?

LORNA: Sit down!

ANNE: What?

LORNA: Over there.

(ANNE *sits in the chair at which the camera is pointing.* LORNA *switches on the equipment and starts fiddling with it.*)

ANNE: What's that camera doing?

(ANNE's *live image appears on the screen.*)

Lorna!

LORNA: I want to try something out.

ANNE: Try what out?

LORNA: Just a little screen test. For the show.

ANNE: (*Getting up*) You've planned all this!

LORNA: It's only an idea.

ANNE: In secret. You've been plotting it!

LORNA: It's only a video, Anne! For God's sake! It's not wired up to Crystal Palace!

ANNE: I don't like it. You should have told me.

LORNA: I just want an idea of how someone who didn't make it would look. Talking about their experience. You and Grant keep telling me to take it seriously. You know what it's like.

ANNE: Yes, but I've got . . . You know how I feel.

LORNA: That's exactly what'll make it real. An audience isn't going to identify with some friendly old nun saying how hard it is. They need someone like you.

(ANNE *considers.*)

Just sit down a minute.

ANNE: (*Sitting down and seeing her image on the screen*) Oh, God, Lorna! I look stupid!

LORNA: Forget the camera. Forget it's there.

ANNE: How can I do that?

LORNA: Relax!

ANNE: It's all right for you. You're not looking at it.

LORNA: Just say a few words.

ANNE: I was born at a very early age . . .

LORNA: No, seriously. How would you do the show? If you were me?

ANNE: Well . . . I'd do it very simply.

LORNA: Yes?

ANNE: Put the camera on them and let them talk. Just that. And if there's a silence . . .

(*Pause.*)

LORNA: Like this?

ANNE: If there's a silence, keep it. (*Beat.*) No, Lorna, turn it off!

LORNA: (*Turning it off*) You look good, you know. Your idea's a bit Grant-ish, but you look good.

ANNE: Those voice-overs and reverses are like smoke. You want time to contemplate their faces. To stay with them. To feel when it's over as if you've met them. Been in the same room, been affected by them. (*Beat.*) I've never been here at this time.

LORNA: It's completely different at night. You have the run of the place. I go sit in other people's offices sometimes and turn the lights on. Not to pry. Just to sit in someone else's chair. Use an unfamiliar telephone . . .

ANNE: What time do you stay till?

LORNA: Ten, eleven, twelve . . . I sleep here sometimes. Why go home?

ANNE: It is quiet.

LORNA: Yet you can see the traffic crossing the flyover. Life out there doesn't stop. An endless stream of red tail lights disappearing over the incline. But all in the distance. That's the beauty.

ANNE: 'The Habit of Perfection'.

(LORNA *looks at her.*)

It's a poem about the religious life. I thought it'd be a good title.

(LORNA *takes* ANNE'*s hat off and turns the camera on again.*)

LORNA: How did people react when you went in?

ANNE: Hostile, patronizing, threatened, admiring for the wrong reasons . . . One or two understood – ones you least expected to.

LORNA: And six months later you were back.

ANNE: I just stayed in bed all day at first, away from everyone. Friends who'd unburdened their souls on to me six months

38

before, thinking they'd never see me again, were too embarrassed to come round. My parents were wonderful though. Relieved it hadn't worked out apart from anything else. And slowly I started to get back into things . . .

LORNA: Invested in a double bed, I hope?

ANNE: You keep talking about sex. It was simple things that were difficult. Not having enough time to do what you wanted. Having to take orders from people you didn't respect.

LORNA: And loneliness?

ANNE: You just had to live with it. Everyone lives with something.

LORNA: Do they?

ANNE: Well, when I told you that PA didn't want to work with you . . . It can't have been news.

LORNA: No.

ANNE: And you've heard those messages on your answering machine?

(LORNA *looks at her.*)

LORNA: Gwen. My old PA.

ANNE: You live with that.

LORNA: (*Turns camera off.*) I didn't choose it.

ANNE: You've still got to live with it.

LORNA: It's not the same.

ANNE: But it's not something . . .

LORNA: (*Interrupting*) All right, I live with it! I don't need telling that!

ANNE: Look, I didn't mean . . .

LORNA: (*Interrupting*) I know you didn't mean. I know. (*Beat.*) I suppose I want to find things out without them touching me. Television style. Too much to do in too little time, so no time to go deep. No time to think about the outside world. Pressure from above to steer clear of sensitive issues. It's a wonderful job, Anne.

ANNE: No time to think about being alone?

LORNA: Yes. If you like.

ANNE: (*Beat.*) Have you got a man, or. . . ?

LORNA: (*Laughs briefly.*) If you can count Jevon. Don't bother with the surprised look. Yes, I live with it, Anne. (*Beat.*) You can help this show.

ANNE: Yes.

LORNA: Think about it. Over the holiday. I want this one to be different.

ANNE: I'd like to.

LORNA: We'll talk after Christmas. Yes?

ANNE: Yes.

(ANNE *smiles*. LORNA *smiles back*.)

ACT II

SCENE 8

Lorna's office. Two weeks later. Early January. Morning.
CAROLINE *is typing.* GRANT *has just arrived.*

GRANT: Good Christmas?

CAROLINE: Wonderful, yeah. You?

GRANT: Oh, in between the six hundred and one drinks parties we had to go to it was quite relaxing. Did you go up to Norfolk?

CAROLINE: Down, mm. It was lovely. I.went to loads of parties too. Saw all my old friends, had all the family round for Christmas dinner, hunting on Boxing Day . . .

GRANT: I'm sure the fox was delighted.

CAROLINE: They do enjoy it actually. (*Beat.*) Went to midnight mass.

GRANT: Really?

CAROLINE: I quite like it actually. I think the old idea of a church being the centre of a community was a good one. Specially in the country. Doesn't matter if you believe or not. And it's what Christmas is about, after all, isn't it? Religion?

GRANT: Ethno-anthropologically, I suppose it is, yeah.

CAROLINE: I think Christmas has become too commercialized. People have forgotten what it really means.

GRANT: You been doing some thinking about this? (*Beat.*) You must quite like the nun project then?

CAROLINE: Well . . . There's religion and religion, isn't there? In the olden days it was quite important, but to do it now . . . It's a bit extreme. But it gives you something, religion. You need something, don't you? Specially these days.

GRANT: What do you need?

CAROLINE: Well, they say we live in an age of doubt . . .

GRANT: Do they?

CAROLINE: Yeah. And they say rules are made to be broken. But you still need rules in the first place. I think, anyway.

GRANT: (*Beat.*) Do you like breaking rules, Caroline?

(CAROLINE *smiles and shrugs*.)
Hmm?
CAROLINE: Sometimes.
GRANT: (*Moving closer to her*) What's this you're typing?
CAROLINE: Letter.
GRANT: Anything interesting?
CAROLINE: It's a circular to all the magistrates' courts in
London.
(GRANT *picks up her notepad*.)
It's in shorthand.
GRANT: I can read shorthand, you know.
CAROLINE: You're such an all-round man.
GRANT: You don't believe me, do you?
(CAROLINE *shrugs*.)
Shall I read it out?
CAROLINE: If you like.
GRANT: You might think I'm bluffing if I don't.
CAROLINE: You'd better read it then.
GRANT: (*Reads*:) 'Dear Madam, We are intending to make a
television documentary about a woman magistrate as part of
our acclaimed series *Women at Work*.' Shall I go on?
CAROLINE: Is this how you knock the ladies dead, Grant?
Showing off your secretarial skills?
GRANT: Aren't you impressed?
CAROLINE: I tell you what would impress me.
GRANT: Oh? What?
(*In an atmosphere of sexual anticipation* CAROLINE *gets up and
stands next to* GRANT. *Short pause*.)
CAROLINE: You can stop looking up my skirt in convent
bedrooms for a start. Please.
GRANT: (*Beat, then smiles*.) Fair enough.
(*She sits down and he goes back to his desk. Enter* JEVON.)
JEVON: Good morning, children!
CAROLINE: Morning!
JEVON: (*To* GRANT) Everywhere.
GRANT: Morning, Jevon.
JEVON: Or is it afternoon? (*Looks at his watch*.) No, I just qualify.
Happy New Year, anyway. Message for you, Caroline.

42

(*He gives her a note.*)

CAROLINE: Oh!

JEVON: Moving in rather exotic circles all of a sudden, aren't we?

(CAROLINE *looks embarrassed.*)

I thought they had the wrong extension at first. I was going to have them transferred but then I thought Caroline wears such nice flannelette . . . I thought I'd . . . Where's Lorna?

CAROLINE: She's with Anne somewhere.

JEVON: Is she indeed? No crucifixes on the wall yet though? How was the nunnery?

GRANT: It was very interesting.

JEVON: I thought someone might have turned it into a novel by now. *Four Go to Pendle Abbey.* Did you find lots of secret passages, Caroline?

CAROLINE: I had to come back on the Saturday. There weren't enough beds.

JEVON: No room at the inn, eh? So what. . . ?

CAROLINE: Lorna shared with Anne.

JEVON: Did she really? Hmm. Lorna and Anne . . . And how do you feel about it now, Grant? It was your idea.

GRANT: Well, I . . .

JEVON: (*Interrupting*) Three months in . . . Is it coming out pretty much as you saw it?

GRANT: I think as soon as we get . . .

JEVON: (*Interrupting*) What do you think's going to be the end of it all?

GRANT: The end?

JEVON: The end, mm.

GRANT: (*Beat.*) What do you mean, 'the end'?

JEVON: We don't want it to be too religious, for example, do we? We're not on any hobby-horses. It's women at work after all, not women at prayer. I think we should keep the religion at a distance. Tangential rather than central to use the jargon, hmm?

GRANT: I think we've got to put religion wherever it's best going to serve the programme, actually.

JEVON: Oh, do you?

GRANT: It's a programme about someone who gave up a career most of us can only dream about for an esoteric way of life. We've got to look at that life.

JEVON: My point exactly. It's a show about people for whom religion is important, not religion as such.

GRANT: But we've got to show respect for that subject matter if it's not going to be the usual condescension. And we've got to look at the implications of her decision – how it affects us, how it challenges us.

JEVON: 'Challenge?'

GRANT: People should come away asking serious questions about how they run their lives, what their priorities are, the success ethos the media swamp us with. I think it could be disturbing in a quite radical way.

JEVON: I see. Well . . . I've no doubt Lorna'll be able to blend all that into her own vision of the programme. I'll have to talk to her about it later. No, that's very interesting . . . Anne's been filling her in on the background, I take it?

GRANT: I expect so.

JEVON: She's all right, is she – Lorna?

GRANT: Far as I know.

JEVON: Tell her I popped in. (*To* CAROLINE) Hmm? Pretty thing? Tell her I popped in.
(*Exit* JEVON. CAROLINE *takes her letter and some other mail and exits. The phone rings and* GRANT *answers it.*)

GRANT: (*Into phone*) Social Features? Hi. (*Writes.*) Mm. No. No. (*Laughs briefly.*) No, very uncool! I'd have to look at the transcript, Billy, can you. . . ?
(*He searches.*)

LORNA: (*Off*) Last time I sat in that bar at lunchtime a sound recordist nearly threw a dart in my foot.
(*Enter* LORNA *and* ANNE *with yoghurty things for lunch, and a book.*)

ANNE: It makes your clothes smell too.
(LORNA, GRANT *and* ANNE *acknowledge each other.*)

LORNA: (*Leading* ANNE *to her desk*) Let's do it here – it's easier.

GRANT: (*Into phone, having found the transcript*) Tell you what –

I'll come down. No, I'll bring it with me. We can have a jar if you like . . . OK. Bye. (*Puts phone down, picks up the transcript and starts to leave; then to* LORNA *and* ANNE, *ironically*) Happy New Year!

ANNE: Happy New Year!

(LORNA *smiles. Exit* GRANT. LORNA *and* ANNE *have their lunch.*)

LORNA: Show me those photos again.

(ANNE *gives her the book.*)

They do have beautiful faces.

ANNE: Some of them are beautiful. Some are horrible old pigs. They're like anybody else. They don't become saints overnight just because they wear strange clothes and spend all their time praying.

LORNA: It would be wonderful if you'd be in the show.

ANNE: (*Beat.*) I don't want to be the failed nun who became a television person. I don't want it to affect my career. Sounds selfish, I know . . .

LORNA: I'm glad you're ambitious. Perhaps if you'd believed in yourself before you wouldn't have needed to run off to a convent.

ANNE: Yes . . . I had another reason. There was a man. I know it's a cliché . . .

LORNA: Ah, yes. Love is first flirtation, then mess.

ANNE: I thought I'd got over it at the time, but looking back . . . I remember dreading the weekends for ages afterwards.

LORNA: Oh, yes!

ANNE: A woman with ringless fingers putting portions for one in a supermarket trolley. Trying not to stare at the arty-looking man with the nice shirts. Hoping if I dropped my butter at the check-out he might pick it up for me . . .

LORNA: At which point you'd pretend not to notice him discreetly taking in your body.

(ANNE *looks at her.*)

Assuming he wasn't gay, of course, which the nice ones usually are. (*Beat.*) How about turning down dinner invitations because you knew it'd all be couples?

ANNE: That's right!

LORNA: 'Did you like the film?' – 'John did, I didn't.'
   (ANNE *smiles*.)
   'Excuse me, everyone. I'm single – I do apologize – but I've
   just discovered the cure for cancer.' – 'How jolly clever of
   you, Lorna!' says my neighbour, looking across at her
   husband as if to say, 'Curious, isn't it, darling – what
   people get up to to compensate for being alone?'
ANNE: (*Laughs*.) And I hated going for walks on my own on
   Sunday afternoons.
LORNA: Oh, my God! Hampstead Heath! Yellow wellingtons!
ANNE: And kites!
LORNA: 'Don't go *too* near the water, Tamsen!'
   (*They laugh*.)
ANNE: Sunday evenings were my favourites. Five days of work
   to look forward to.
LORNA: 'Thou shalt on no account embarrass thy friends by
   admitting to being lonely.'
   (*Pause*.)
ANNE: Were you lonely at school?
LORNA: School*s*. My dear father was in the army and he kept
   moving me, so I was never in the same one long enough to
   settle.
ANNE: What about holidays?
LORNA: God forbid!
   (*The phone rings and* ANNE *answers it*.)
   I've still got the taste of Christmas in my mouth.
ANNE: (*Into phone*) Social Features? Oh, hello. Yes, she is.
   (*Handing* LORNA *the phone*) It's Jevon.
   (LORNA *starts in mock terror and signals to* ANNE *that she
   won't speak to him. They both have to stifle an attack of the
   giggles*.)
   (*Into phone*) Hello, Jevon? She seems to have gone. Do you
   want me to look? Erm . . . Well, she might be in the
   Ladies. No?
LORNA: He's already checked.
ANNE: (*Into phone*) OK. I'll tell her. Yes. Bye. (*Puts phone
   down, laughing*.) He knew you were here.
LORNA: I don't care. He can go fish.

(*Their laughter subsides.*)

I can understand those sisters, turning their backs on it all.

ANNE: It's not that easy.

LORNA: 'The Habit of Perfection' . . .

ANNE: Do you like it?

(LORNA *smiles, and there is a moment of quiet rapport between them.*)

When's your rough-cut?

LORNA: Hell! Is that the time? I said I'd be over there by one. (*Getting up and getting ready to go*) Give them a ring, could you, and say I've been delayed?

(*Enter* CAROLINE.)

CAROLINE: Oh, Lorna! Jevon was looking for you.

LORNA: What was he wearing? Bow tie, safari jacket or Bri-Nylon roll-neck?

CAROLINE: He was asking about Pendle.

LORNA: Tell him it's a place where women live very happily without men. I'll see you both tomorrow.

CAROLINE *and* ANNE: Bye. (*Etc.*)

(*Exit* LORNA.)

CAROLINE: (*Getting her coat*) She was begging me not to leave her alone there two weeks ago. Offering me a place on the PAs' course.

ANNE: (*Dialling*) Have you had any luck with that?

(CAROLINE *snorts and exits.*)

(*Into phone*) Seven two one, please.

(*Enter* JEVON *with a tea and a chocolate biscuit. He looks round for* LORNA *then winks at* ANNE *with benign insincerity. She smiles back.*)

JEVON: (*Whispers*) No Lorna?

(ANNE *shakes her head and* JEVON *raises his eyes upwards.*)

ANNE: (*Into phone*) Oh, Piers? It's Anne Fielding. Hello. Lorna's been delayed, I'm afraid. Well, she's just left, so . . . Quarter past-ish, yes – something like that. OK. Sorry. Bye.

(*She puts phone down.*)

JEVON: Producer's run?

ANNE: *Ladies of the Street*, yes. She'd just gone when you rang.

JEVON: Just my luck. Oh, well . . . (*Beat.*) She *is* doing some ever so interesting work.

ANNE: Lorna?

(JEVON *shakes his head solemnly to show how impressed he is. He breaks off a piece of biscuit and puts it to his mouth.*)

JEVON: (*Remembering his manners*) Sorry, Anne! Do you. . . ? (*He offers her a piece of biscuit.*)

ANNE: (*Declining, pointing to the remains of lunch*) I've just had . . .

JEVON: I'm trying to give lunches up. But I do like something lovely about this time. Keep the morale going. I find the day catches up with you later on otherwise. Bad for the figure, I know, but yes . . . Lorna's been telling me all the wonderful things that are going on in here. Street cleaners, magistrates, nuns . . . You've popped up at a very interesting time.

ANNE: It's exciting, yes.

(*Pause.*)

JEVON: I do like those pop-up cards, don't you? I think they're great fun. Yes, it's going to look very impressive on your c.v. Have you thought about what you might move on to next?

ANNE: Not really. Bit early for that. Main thing is to get these projects out on time and make them as well as we can.

JEVON: Oh, absolutely, absolutely. On the other hand, no time like the present for planning ahead. Gavin Cooke, for example. I know he was looking for someone to help him on his European painting project.

ANNE: In the spring?

JEVON: Arts Features, yes. Do you know Gavin? Cutting my own throat suggesting it perhaps. No one likes losing a quality PA. Talent shouldn't be hidden under bushels though . . . We like to see people get on. (*Beat.*) You won't tell Lorna I've been likening her to a bushel?

ANNE: No, no.

JEVON: What is a bushel anyway, I wonder?

ANNE: It's a water carrier.

JEVON: Is it really? How absolutely fascinating. No, think about it.

ANNE: OK.

JEVON: I'll be seeing him later this week, Gavin. I'll have a word
in his ear if you like. I mean he may've already found
someone, but a nudge in the right direction . . . Never did
any harm. Mmm?
ANNE: No. Thank you.
(JEVON *smiles and exits.*)

SCENE 9

A week later. Early/mid January. Morning. JEVON, *holding a
document, is talking to* LORNA.

JEVON: Lorna, it's all very well to talk about shaking people up at
the NFT or the Academy – people expect it there. This is
television. It's going into people's homes. I can just hear
those sets being switched over up and down the country five
or six minutes in.
LORNA: They may switch over.
JEVON: But it's such a shame! I don't know what's got into you.
(*Looks at document.*) No voice-overs, no reverse angles. 'A
searching look at her decision to renounce and go beyond
what most of us would be only too happy to settle for . . .'
You haven't gone religious, have you?
LORNA: Who knows?
JEVON: Heaven prevent!
LORNA: Don't blaspheme!
JEVON: What is your game, Lorna? It's so earnest!
LORNA: There's no game. I just want to try something different.
I wanted to do it in black and white . . .
JEVON: Black and white!
LORNA: We spend all our time worrying about people switching
over. We put tricksy devices in to make it more 'interesting'.
We end up patronizing the subject, the people; we insult the
audience's intelligence – it's no wonder they switch over.
People are hungry for programmes that don't treat them like
idiots. They *want* us to take things seriously.
JEVON: Well, don't we? I thought we cared very deeply about the
things we do. It's Social Features – the department that got a

49

public inquiry launched into that old folk's home in Manchester.

LORNA: I know . . .

JEVON: We have that tradition. I just don't want people to be thrown off kilter if we go too far out in the treatment and start making Grant-ish statements about dropping out of the rat race. (*Beat.*) And another thing. Billy tells me you're leaving all the bad language in *Ladies of the Street*.

LORNA: Only where they talk about the local workmen shouting at them.

JEVON: You know very well it won't be let through. Especially the 'cunt'. They don't like 'cunt' at Television Centre. You can have the odd 'shit' if you like, or even a quick 'fuck' if it's absolutely essential, but 'cunt''s something else. They're very particular about 'cunt'.

LORNA: So are women. That's why it's staying in. (*Beat.*) By the way, I won't be coming to the theatre on Friday.

JEVON: I thought it was *next* weekend your mother was coming?

LORNA: It is. (*Beat.*) Jevon, I'm not sleeping with you any more.

JEVON: Oh?

LORNA: You know I haven't been too happy about things recently . . .

JEVON: I thought you'd worked out all that uncertainty?

LORNA: I have. And I'm certain it's over.

(JEVON *stares at her.*)

My best years don't exactly stretch out in front of me. I can't go on depending on a married man whose priorities are quite understandably to someone else.

JEVON: I've told you before, I'm only waiting . . .

LORNA: (*Interrupting*) You have no intention of leaving her. We both know that. I need to get back my self-respect. If that means being on my own then so be it. We have a good professional relationship here. There's no reason why that shouldn't continue.

JEVON: It's that Anne, isn't it?

LORNA: (*Laughs briefly.*) 'That' Anne? (*Beat.*) Jevon, it's me.

JEVON: No, but on the programmes. She's turning your mind.

LORNA: She's not a Moonie.

JEVON: It's where it's all leading that worries me. Sooner it's spring, the better.

LORNA: What's happening then?

JEVON: She's going back into the pool.

LORNA: She is bloody not!

JEVON: Excuse me, but it's not up to you where PAs go when their projects are finished.

LORNA: She wouldn't want to work with John Rice again.

JEVON: Who's saying anything about John Rice? Gavin Cooke's looking for someone enterprising for his European painting extravaganza in April.

LORNA: So?

JEVON: I think you might not be as close to what she wants as you think. She's an ambitious girl. She's failed once in her life . . . He's got twelve fifty-five-minute slots, you know – Gavin. Travelling round Europe. Tempting proposition for anybody.

LORNA: You said Lyall was giving me some longer slots . . .

JEVON: I said he was thinking about it. Wouldn't be till next year if he did.

LORNA: Well, I'm glad she's in such demand. Good luck to her. If she wants to work with all these wise and wonderful men. I'm not married to her. (*Beat.*) She's said she wants to do all this?

JEVON: You pick things up at my end of the corridor that don't always filter down to the lower reaches . . . You may have to make the most of her while you can. Gavin's already starting pre-production. It could be any day now . . .

(LORNA *considers briefly, then gets up.*)

LORNA: Nice try, Jevon.

JEVON: Who's trying?

LORNA: You are, darling. Very hard and rather cheaply. I'm sorry you've lost your occasional piece on the side but you'll have to be a little more sophisticated than that.

(JEVON *shrugs disingenuously.*)

I must say I'd have expected rather more lightness of touch. Perhaps it's the early hour. Place feels different to you probably, does it, before ten in the morning?

JEVON: Who's feeling piqued now?

LORNA: (*Smiles*.) The words are yours.

(*Exit* LORNA, *leaving* JEVON *thoughtful. Enter* GRANT.)

GRANT: (*Surprised*) Hi.

JEVON: Morning, Grant.

GRANT: Looking for Lorna?

JEVON: Hmm? No, I was just perusing the . . . (*He picks something up off Lorna's desk.*)

GRANT: In the loo probably.

JEVON: . . . state of play . . . How many were they, by the way? Do you know?

GRANT: Who?

JEVON: The Australians!

GRANT: Oh! I don't know. I don't listen.

JEVON: No, of course . . . I keep a little transistor in my office. Specially for winter tours. I think I'll just go have a quick ripple on Radio Three. See if the tail wagged. Hope to God it didn't!

(JEVON *smiles and exits.* ANNE *and* CAROLINE *meet him on their way in.*)

ANNE: Morning, Jevon!

JEVON: (*Off*) Morning, girls!

(ANNE *is wearing less dowdy clothes than we've so far seen her in, and is carrying a package.*)

ANNE: Hi!

GRANT: How was the recce?

ANNE: Fine.

GRANT: Good hotel?

ANNE: Would you believe 'The Abbey'?

CAROLINE: Oh, no!

ANNE: With a restaurant called 'The Refectory'?

GRANT: In Gothic script, I hope?

ANNE: It's quite nice actually. Two star. Family business, so it's not too formal. And so quiet! I slept like a log.

GRANT: As long as there's a bar.

ANNE: 'The Cloisters' is licensed till midnight for the convenience of our patrons.

(GRANT *and* CAROLINE *groan.*)

(*Opening the package*) I bet this is the invitations. It is.

CAROLINE: Oh, let's have a look! Oh, they're nice.

GRANT: Hey, is this story true about David Miles doing more re-shoots in Glasgow?

CAROLINE: It's what Geraldine said. (*To* ANNE) While you were away.

GRANT: She's got to give it to me if it is. Bloody hell, it was my idea!

ANNE: (*To* CAROLINE) Have you been to a preview before?

CAROLINE: Not at BAFTA.

ANNE: They're fun.

> (*Enter* LORNA.)

> (*Not seeing her*) All the critics come. You can do a bit of hobnobbing. (*Sees* LORNA.) Oh, Lorna, are you doing a press release for this?

> (*She gives her an invitation card.*)

LORNA: You're back looking smart.

ANNE: Oh . . . I bought it in the sales. I thought it'd be more colourful.

LORNA: Than your cardigan, yes, I suppose it is. Suits the upwardly mobile image, certainly. No wonder it's taken you three days to sort out the accommodation. (*Looks at card.*) They'll do. Thirtieth of Jan. What's that? Three weeks. You ordered the wine, didn't you?

ANNE: Case of each.

LORNA: Can't have them going in sober. Cashews and olives for Connie Sayer or she'll do a hatchet job. And the seat nearest the back for Richard Kooning – he doesn't like people to see him picking his nose. And take these expense claims down to Accounts, will you? They're querying them as usual.

ANNE: Now?

LORNA: No time like the present, Anne. You don't have to book secret appointments with the men in that department, you know.

> (*Exit* ANNE, *puzzled and slightly hurt*. GRANT *and* CAROLINE *exchange looks.*)

GRANT: (*To* LORNA) I've written to Sister Margaret again. I'm going down to see her next week.

LORNA: I hope you'll both be very happy. Did you speak to Billy?

GRANT: Not since last week.

LORNA: He's found more contradictions in the voice-overs on *Ladies of the Street*.

GRANT: It's all in my report. He can check.

LORNA: Help him sort it out, will you? You know what he's like.

GRANT: (*Reluctantly reaching for phone*) I'm going to try and persuade her to give us more time.

LORNA: Be quicker to slip down. He's having one of his bad days. Stammering just talking to himself over coffee. His elastic'll go completely if he has to start explaining things over the phone.

(*Exit* GRANT, *grudgingly*.)

(*To* CAROLINE) What's wrong with you? You look as if you've just commissioned an unknown director. Reminds me – I must check how Philip Holland's thing's coming along.

CAROLINE: Lorna, I know you said no before but it's about the trainee PAs' course in March . . . Only you said at the convent you'd get me on the next one.

LORNA: (*Searching for something*) Did I?

CAROLINE: Well, not in so many words. The thing is, they still have vacancies . . .

LORNA: What is it? A boarding house? You've only been here ten months.

CAROLINE: Twelve and a half.

LORNA: Caroline, you are beginning to get boring. When I think you're ready I will give you a reference. Until then you are my secretary. All right? (*Still searching*) Where's my internal directory?

CAROLINE: Oh, Melda popped in to borrow it. She's lost her new one.

LORNA: Then you'd better get it back, hadn't you?

(*Exit* CAROLINE. LORNA *fumes alone. Enter* ANNE *with the accounts file*.)

ANNE: There's nobody there. I'll have to take them down later.

(*Pause.*)

LORNA: (*Pleasantly*) I hear you're thinking of moving on to better things?

ANNE: Oh?

LORNA: Or have I got it wrong? Jevon said you might be going to work for Gavin Cooke.

ANNE: (*Embarrassed*) He mentioned it.

LORNA: Attractive proposition.

ANNE: I suppose it is, yes.

LORNA: Big producer, big series. Give you just the lift you need.

ANNE: It would be exciting. Not that I'm unhappy here.

LORNA: No?

ANNE: You know I'm not.

LORNA: Just as well I keep my ear to the ground and find these things out for myself. I thought we were both committed to this project, but I'm wrong obviously.

ANNE: I only found out about it . . .

LORNA: (*Interrupting*) If you can give me a date some time . . .

ANNE: It's only an idea, Lorna! I thought if Jevon was suggesting it . . .

LORNA: Oh? What did you think?

ANNE: Well, I know you and Jevon . . . you told me that night you and Jevon were . . .

LORNA: What I told you in confidence has absolutely no bearing on what goes on in this office.

ANNE: I know!

LORNA: You may be happy to bare *your* soul about all the boyfriend troubles you'd been having that made you turn to religion but I prefer to keep my own affairs rather more private.

(ANNE *looks hurt.*)

If everyone felt a vocation when they got jilted the convents would be full to bursting. Specially ones near television studios. Have you drawn up a list of invites?

ANNE: I haven't had time.

LORNA: Do it before you go.

ANNE: Yes, of course.

(*Tense pause as they go about their separate business.* LORNA *is upset at having upset* ANNE. *She takes an ancient packet of cigarettes from a drawer and smokes one briefly.*)

LORNA: (*Finally*) You say Jevon suggested all this?

ANNE: Yes! It wasn't me.

LORNA: When did he speak to you?

ANNE: Last week. I didn't mention it . . .

LORNA: (*Interrupting*) What did he say?

ANNE: It all sounded so provisional. He said he was very impressed with the work you were doing . . .

LORNA: He said what?

ANNE: That working with you would look good on my c.v. . . . Then he said Gavin was looking for someone and was I interested?

LORNA: And you said yes. Who wouldn't?

ANNE: I said the main thing was to do my projects for you before thinking about moving on. He said he'd have a word with Gavin anyway. That was it.
(LORNA *takes this in, not finding it easy, but slowly calming down.*)

LORNA: Do you want to move?

ANNE: I hadn't been thinking . . .

LORNA: (*Interrupting*) No, but do you want to?

ANNE: I don't specially want to, no. But if I did get the chance to work with Gavin . . .

LORNA: You'd take it.

ANNE: I'd be crazy not to.

LORNA: Did he mention all this might mean your going before the shoot?

ANNE: How could I do that?

LORNA: He told me it could be any day now.

ANNE: He was talking about the spring. I can't leave now.

LORNA: You can if an executive producer invites you to.

ANNE: But we're almost there. I want to see it through.

LORNA: My show's not going to give you the same boost as Gavin's. You know that, don't you? You'd be crazy to pass up on it.

ANNE: What would you do?

56

LORNA: I'd have to manage. (*Beat.*) I'll be OK. You think about yourself. (*Pause.*) I'm sorry I barked at you.

ANNE: It's all right.

LORNA: It's not all right actually. It's unforgivable. It's bad for me apart from anything else. I'm supposed to be giving up biting people. Even Jevon.
(*They smile. Enter* JEVON *carrying a letter and looking pleased with himself, followed by* CAROLINE *with the directory.*)

JEVON: Do I hear my ears burning? How is the new wave of the British documentary movement this morning? Hmm? The engine room of the *nouvelle vague*?

LORNA: (*Taking the directory*) Steaming ahead merrily, thank you.

JEVON: I bring good tidings for a change. (*Throws letter on Lorna's desk and looks at* ANNE.) Never let it be said that people's careers are held back in large institutions such as this.

LORNA: (*Passing it to* ANNE) It's confirmation of your move.

ANNE: What?

LORNA: Congratulations.

ANNE: When do I go?

LORNA: End of the week.

ANNE: Oh.

CAROLINE: Where are you going?

ANNE: Gavin Cooke.

CAROLINE: Wow! Well done! You kept that quiet.

ANNE: Jevon arranged it.

JEVON: I'm sorry it leaves you without a PA at such short notice. It's earlier than I thought, but if she hadn't made the move now . . . Gavin was looking for someone fairly urgently . . . It's a big project.

LORNA: That's all right.

JEVON: I'll try and speed things up in the pool to get you someone. I know you're only four weeks away from shooting . . .

LORNA: I'm not sure we're going to need anyone actually.

JEVON: Oh?

LORNA: Caroline knows as much as anyone about this project. I

57

think she could handle it. If she wanted to, that is. What do you say, Caroline?

CAROLINE: Well . . .

JEVON: She isn't qualified, is she? Sorry, Caroline, but you haven't done the course, have you?

LORNA: I can help her. Why bring anyone in? Time's so short. It'd take us from now to the shoot to teach someone new. If you're prepared for a couple of months' hard work, Caroline . . .

CAROLINE: Yeah. Sure.

JEVON: (*To* LORNA) Well, if you're prepared to take the risk.

LORNA: Which I am.

JEVON: What about David? He's going to want someone who knows what they're doing. No disrespect to you of course, Caroline, but . . .

LORNA: David's extremely unlikely to be available for this one.

JEVON: Oh? What. . . ?

LORNA: (*Holding up a letter*) One of his drug addicts has gone to a rehabilitation centre for some new therapy. They've put back transmission dates so he can do re-shoots.

JEVON: Who's going to direct it then?

(*Enter* GRANT. LORNA *looks at him.* JEVON *follows* LORNA's *gaze.*)

SCENE 10

A week later. Mid January. Afternoon. GRANT *and* CAROLINE *are working on the schedule.* CAROLINE *sits in Anne's old chair and is using a word processor.*

CAROLINE: What was Sister Margaret like?

GRANT: Polite, wary . . . Didn't say much. I felt I was on trial.

CAROLINE: Obviously passed.

GRANT: I was just honest with her. She knew I'd only gone down to ask her for more time – I didn't try to pretend otherwise. I told her why. Told her how we wanted to do the programme. She went away and thought about it, then told the Reverend Mother.

58

CAROLINE: Does that mean you're not going to be using those interviews with Anne any more?

GRANT: What interviews?

CAROLINE: Lorna videoed Anne talking about her time in the convent.

GRANT: Really? (*Beat.*) Where are we up to, anyway?

CAROLINE: Friday the eighth, 10 am to 1 pm: refectory . . . (*Enter* LORNA.)

LORNA: How's it going?

GRANT: Fine. We've more or less done the first week.

LORNA: (*Looking*) Yes . . . Good . . . Yes . . . *Two* night shoots?

GRANT: Exterior of them going to prayers, and the soup kitchen in Ipswich.

LORNA: Budget won't run. You can have one at the most.

GRANT: OK.

LORNA: Have you got copyright clearance for the Dreyer film?

GRANT: We're looking into it.

LORNA: That extra time with Sister Margaret could transform the whole scope of the thing. Well done!

GRANT: I asked her about taking some shots of her parents' house – she says she doesn't mind.

LORNA: (*Nods.*) Uh huh. When are you going to do it?

GRANT: Second week sometime.

LORNA: Don't forget to allow travelling time.

GRANT: It'll only be down the road!

LORNA: Our friends in the ACTT won't see it like that. And they'll need half a day to get into Ipswich for the soup-kitchen sequence.

GRANT: Three miles?

LORNA: And half a day to get back.

GRANT: Do we fit any shooting in between all this travelling around?

LORNA: Love, we might be trying to make an earth-shattering work of art. To them it's just another job. Directing is a game. Being an artist is only half of it. The other half's planning and keeping people happy. You're doing very well but keep an eye on the practicals.

(*Pause.*)

GRANT: Yeah, OK. (*Smiles.*) Bloody institution!

LORNA: Now now! Don't let Uncle Mac hear you using language like that!

GRANT: I'll go check out that copyright.

(*Exit* GRANT.)

LORNA: Enjoying it?

CAROLINE: (*Enthusiastic*) So different when you're involved.

LORNA: You won't forget that typing for the magistrate show?

CAROLINE: I'll stay late if I have to.

LORNA: I must catch up on a few things myself, tonight. (*Beat.*) We could go for an Italian after, if you're free.

CAROLINE: Oh. Er . . . Well, I said I'd ring Neville.

LORNA: Oh, all right.

CAROLINE: I haven't seen him for a couple of days . . .

LORNA: No, it was just a thought. I must try and get an early night, actually . . . (*Listening*) Is that the trolley?

CAROLINE: She's been. Do you want something?

LORNA: Could you? I'd go, but . . .

CAROLINE: Black?

LORNA: No sugar.

(*Enter* JEVON *on the back of this.*)

JEVON: And I'll have my usual if you please, Caroline. Sliver of milk without. (*Gives her money.*) *Grazie!*

CAROLINE: *Prego.*

(JEVON *looks at her, slightly taken aback by her response.* CAROLINE *smiles and exits.*)

JEVON: So where is the young David Lean if he's in such control of everything?

LORNA: He's just gone down the corridor. Calm down!

JEVON: And he's done the scheduling?

LORNA: He's winning. What are you afraid of?

(JEVON *splutters.*)

No, seriously. What?

JEVON: The ever-so-slight possibility that Grant is not experienced enough to be thrown into directing a difficult project this far advanced. That somewhere between his actual ability to direct and his worthy but rather misplaced

60

ideas about the art of the medium he will, to put it mildly, prang. That at best we'll have a show that's so botched it'll need a miracle of editing to knock it into any kind of shape, and, at worst, no show at all, and fifty thousand quidsworth of explaining to do.

LORNA: I think you underestimate him. People have got to start somewhere. I'm keeping an eye on him. If you never risk anything . . .

JEVON: Oh, so it is a risk?

LORNA: Of course it is. What's happened to the department's spirit of inquiry you're so fond of quoting?

JEVON: Nothing's happened. We have every right to be proud of it. All the more reason to keep the ship afloat.

LORNA: I just think Grant deserves a chance. He knows his career's on the line.

JEVON: (*Beat.*) This is all very noble and generous of you, Lorna, I'm sure. But when your little flirtation with altruism is over and you return to the real world, you're going to find yourself high and dry unless you're extremely careful.

LORNA: Oh, Jevon, spare me the pomp!

(JEVON *sees he's getting nowhere. Pause.*)

JEVON: What time is it?

LORNA: Half-three.

JEVON: What have you got on today?

LORNA: Oh . . . bits of this and that.

JEVON: Look, why don't we hop into a cab and go have tea up at Brown's?

(LORNA *looks at him suspiciously.*)

No, I don't mean that. I mean to talk. We are still colleagues. We don't talk often enough these days. Some of our best discussions about work were away from the office, I remember. We shouldn't be fighting all the time – it's not good for the programmes apart from anything else. How about it? Quick skive up to Brown's. Fresh cakes. Turn round the little park at the back of Farm Street, sort a few things out . . . We could be back here by half-five.

LORNA: (*Pause.*) I don't fancy it.

JEVON: I miss our little chats.

61

LORNA: Jevon, I do not want any cake, and I do not see the need to discuss the matter any further.

JEVON: All right. But if your experiment does backfire you could be burning your boats completely.

LORNA: And what if I am? What if I'm thrown out of here on my arse and told never to come back? There's life beyond Television Centre, you know. Real life. Even for spinsters. (*Pause.*)

JEVON: Lorna, you are three weeks away from shooting. I strongly advise you to bring in a new director *now*. Someone who knows what they're doing, who'll deliver on time and within budget, even if it isn't a very inspired piece of work. It'll be better in the long term for everyone. You, him, the series . . .

LORNA: You.

JEVON: Yes, me too. But believe it or not that truly isn't my prime consideration at this point. You're at a very important stage in your career. Don't forget your promotion to longer slots isn't a foregone conclusion by any means, and with Grant at the helm of this one you're jeopardizing your chances considerably. Considerably. Grant is not ready.
(*Enter* CAROLINE *with teas.*)
(*To* LORNA) Think about it.

LORNA: Oh, I will. I am.

JEVON: (*Taking his tea and going*) Afternoon, Caroline.

CAROLINE: Bye.
(*Exit* JEVON. LORNA *is left looking quite shaken.*)
(*Giving* LORNA *her coffee*) You OK?

LORNA: Yes.

CAROLINE: Sure?

LORNA: (*Beat.*) No, I'm fine thanks, Caroline. I'm fine . . .
(*Pause as* LORNA *gathers herself.*)
Let's get on, shall we?

A week later. Mid/late January. Around 9 pm. LORNA *has finished working and is alone in the office. She is edgy and moves around the office doing edgy things, unable to settle at any one of them, yet unable to leave. She eventually replays her answering machine.*

GWEN: (*On tape*) Hello, this is the Thought Police here, Lorna. Just checking up on that evil little mind of yours. Message ends. Byee!

(LORNA *winces.*)

JEVON: (*On tape*) Oh, Lorna, it's Jevon here. Six-thirty Wednesday evening. I'll be working late tonight. Just wondering if you're on your own by any chance and fancied a quick coffee or a bite or something . . . If there's anything on the programme you wanted to talk through – give me a buzz. Hope everything's OK. I'll be here till around nine-thirty. Bye.

(LORNA *looks at her watch and switches off the machine. Enter* GRANT *suddenly.*)

GRANT: Lorna!

LORNA: (*Jumps.*) Jesus! Grant! Where've you been?

GRANT: Back down to the abbey. I left a tape here. (*Searching*) Have you seen it?

LORNA: What've you been doing since last Thursday?

GRANT: Lots of red felt-tip on the back. I know – I've hardly touched base, I've been so busy.

LORNA: Not on the schedule, you haven't. We've only got two weeks, you know.

GRANT: Lorna, I have got some wonderful news.

LORNA: What?

GRANT: I saw Sister Margaret again this afternoon. I'd been running through what I'm going to be asking her when she suddenly started talking about her advertising days. At one point in the seventies she had to handle a contract with one of the major political parties.

LORNA: Which one?

GRANT: She wouldn't say. But she was asked to advise on how to exploit public sympathy after one of their ministers was nearly killed in a car-bomb attack. They were down in the opinion polls at the time and they had a by-election coming up. They wanted her to get maximum mileage out of it to swing things back their way.

LORNA: Why did she tell you all this?

GRANT: It was an example of the kind of thing she had to do.

LORNA: Is she saying that's why she joined the order?

GRANT: No, no. She made that absolutely clear. She didn't want to do it but then pressure from the Board of Directors cos it was a big contract, and she had no option. (*Beat.*) There was something about the way she kept referring to the other ministers she met – she kept using the present tense . . . I'm sure they're still in power.

LORNA: Be careful, Grant. Be very careful.

GRANT: I'm not thinking of making a big number out of it. It's such a brilliant example of how politics uses advertising . . .

LORNA: (*Interrupting*) We're not doing a show about politics.

GRANT: No, but we *are* about the world she got away from.

LORNA: I thought we were making it clear the religious life has nothing to do with escape?

GRANT: I know that, but . . . Yes, we *are*. Listen, I'm not trying to sensationalize the programme . . .

LORNA: Then what are you trying to do?

GRANT: I want to find a way of using it somewhere. It could crystallize everything the show's saying.

LORNA: I think more to the point is the state of the schedule.

GRANT: Let's have a look.

LORNA: (*At the word processor*) Here, for example. Wednesday the thirteenth. Which are you going for? The soup kitchen or the chapel?

GRANT: I was leaving it loose for the time being.

LORNA: You can't leave a decision about a night shoot loose. You're leaving quite a bit in the air as it is. Here and there it doesn't matter, but . . . Look. Here. What sort of footage have you come up with for the jet-set sequence?

GRANT: I thought we could leave that till the edit. I've found loads of useful stuff. We can't make final decisions about everything now.

LORNA: No, but it ought to be looking tighter than this. We
have to send it out next week.

GRANT: Lorna, it'll be ready. (*Beat.*) But what do you say about
the car bomb?

LORNA: I'll have to think about it. If we start upsetting the
people upstairs the whole thing could go under.

GRANT: It could just give it that edge.

(LORNA *looks at him.*)

I've got to get back. (*Finding tape*) Di's having friends
round. I won't even make it for coffee at this rate.

LORNA: Grant!

(*He stops.*)

I want that schedule by Monday. It must be ready.

GRANT: Don't worry. (*Beat.*) You should get home, Lorna. You
look tired. (*Beat.*) I'll see you tomorrow.

LORNA: Goodnight, Grant.

(*Exit* GRANT, *leaving* LORNA *looking worried and alone. She
gets her things together, but still she can't leave. She checks a
telephone number and dials.*)

(*Into phone*) Oh! Is Anne there? Ah! Is that her brother,
or. . . ? Oh, I see. Sorry, my name's Lorna Brooks. Anne
used to work for me. I'm . . . Could you tell her I rang?
Thanks. Not urgent, no. Lorna Brooks. Yes. Bye.

(*She puts the phone down, and after a little more hesitation she
replays the end of the last message on her machine.*)

JEVON: (*On tape*) . . . everything's OK. I'll be here till around
nine-thirty. Bye.

(*She switches off the machine, looks at her watch and considers.
She picks up the internal phone and dials.*)

SCENE 12

The next morning. Mid/late January. LORNA *sits alone, looking
thoughtful. Enter* GRANT *at speed.*

GRANT: (*Taking coat off, etc.*) Hi. Sorry I'm a bit late. I was up
watching this (*indicates videotape*) till three. *Diary of a
Country Priest.* Extraordinary film – do you know it? Such a

65

pity we can't do it in black and white – you get so much
more depth. (*Beat.*) Why's Jevon want to see *Ladies of the
Street* again on Tuesday? He's not going to be able to
change anything in one day.

LORNA: Grant, I'm taking you off the show.

GRANT: What?

LORNA: I'm sorry.

GRANT: Why. . . ?

LORNA: I'm not sure you're ready.

GRANT: What – me? Or the show? What. . . ?

LORNA: Projects that are going well have a certain feel to them
at each stage of pre-production. This one's been pretty
shaky from the beginning. If we were six weeks away from
shooting instead of two . . .

GRANT: Is it the car bomb?

(LORNA *doesn't answer.*)

I don't think I explained that very well. I have no intention
of exploiting it . . .

LORNA: (*Interrupting*) It's not because of that. It's . . . like I say
– you're not quite ready. At this stage a producer needs to
have absolute confidence in the director.

GRANT: So what are you going to do?

LORNA: I called David this morning. He's going to be free after
all. You can do one of your own later on this year.

GRANT: I thought we were together on this one? I thought you
were behind me? Lorna, I can still pull it off. I know I can.
All I need is your support.

LORNA: My decision's a considered one, Grant. You're not
being sacked. We're just putting things back a bit. It'll give
you time to plan one of your own. Perhaps in the autumn. I
don't expect you to thank me for it, but in time to come I
think you'll see it'll all have been for the best. I'll leave you
to think about it, but my decision is final. (*Beat.*) I'm sorry.

(*Exit* LORNA, *leaving* GRANT *shattered. Enter* CAROLINE.)

CAROLINE: They're collecting for old Mr Ansorge in the
canteen. Do you want. . . ? What's wrong?

GRANT: I've been sacked.

CAROLINE: Just now?

(GRANT *nods.*)
Altogether? Why. . . ? What's she. . . ?
GRANT: Fucking bloody sacked. Fucking bloody WOMAANNN!
(*Pause.*)
CAROLINE: Did she say why?
GRANT: Said I wasn't ready. It just seems so sudden. We were
doing OK, weren't we?
CAROLINE: Yes.
GRANT: She never said anything to you?
CAROLINE: Have I been sacked as well?
GRANT: (*Shaking his head, defeated*) Why bother? Why fucking
bother?

SCENE 13

A week later. Late January. Afternoon. LORNA *and* JEVON *are
sitting ready to watch a screening. She sits stony-faced while he flicks
through a document.*
JEVON: Oh good, you've toned down on the Anglo-Saxon as
well. It just provokes a fight otherwise. So unnecessary.
No, it's looking very good now. I'm looking forward to
seeing it. Is Grant around, or. . . ?
LORNA: He's fetching the tape.
JEVON: He's not taking it too badly then?
LORNA: He's over the moon.
JEVON: I know it's humiliating for him but it's best for
everyone. David plays a straight bat. He's coping without
too many problems?
LORNA: He'll be OK.
JEVON: I am glad he's going for a more general look at the
religious life. I must say I'm not sorry to see the back of
that ten-minute interview. I shouldn't think *anyone*'s got
enough of any value to say to merit going on for that long.
Least of all a nun. (*Beat.*) Lorna, I know it's not been easy
for you but you've got to let it go. Stop blaming yourself.
When you're being nominated for awards in three years'
time . . .

67

LORNA: I'll come and thank you, don't worry.

(JEVON *sighs. Enter* GRANT *with the videotape.*)

JEVON: Ah, Grant! Good morning!

GRANT: (*Flat*) Hi.

JEVON: You've brought the finished product, I hope?

GRANT: (*Muttering*) 'Finished' being the operative word.

JEVON: Hmmm?

(*Enter* CAROLINE *as* GRANT *puts the tape in the video machine.*)

Ah, Caroline! Have you got the popcorn?

(CAROLINE *smiles and takes a pew, as* GRANT *sits down as well, smiling slightly manically to himself.*)

Are we ready then? (*To* CAROLINE) You're not going to risk holding hands with me, I don't expect?

GRANT: (*Muttering*) Risks . . .

CAROLINE: (*To* JEVON) You can grab my arm if you get frightened.

JEVON: Well, some of those butch women and their shovels . . .

(*A* WOMAN STREET CLEANER *appears on the screen.*)

NARRATOR: (*On tape*) Five years ago, what you are seeing would, to most English people, have been the kind of thing you read about in the Soviet Union.

(*The image suddenly changes to edited extracts of the video* LORNA *made of* ANNE *in Scene 7.*)

ANNE: (*On tape*) You keep talking about sex, about sex . . .

LORNA: (*On tape*) It's only a video, Anne. For God's sake! It's not wired up to Crystal Palace!

ANNE: (*On tape*) And you've heard those messages on your answering machine?

GWEN: (*On tape*) Hello, Lorna! Long time, no see. Why don't you reply to my messages? Does that executive chair still squeak when you have sex in it?

JEVON: Dear, oh dear!

GWEN: (*On tape*) Lorna, why don't you do everyone a favour and just fuck off, you cow!

ANNE: (*On tape*) I told you that PA didn't want to work with you.

JEVON: I think we've seen enough . . .

68

(LORNA *gets up to turn it off*.)

GWEN: (*On tape*) Lorna, why don't you do everyone a favour. . . ?

(LORNA *switches it off. All eyes on a scared but jubilant* GRANT.)

JEVON: Good job I did want to look through it.

GRANT: Oh, Jevon, didn't you like it? What was wrong? Didn't it deliver? Or did it plateau out rather too early for your liking?

JEVON: Grant . . .

GRANT: You'd have taken the soliloquies out of *Hamlet* you're so obsessed with attention span.

JEVON: I understand how you're feeling . . .

GRANT: And I apologize for the language. I agree with you – we should keep obscenity off our screens at all costs. How about the news that only gives half the picture? Or the sitcoms that drip sexist, racist gags? They're the real obscenities. 'Fuck' never killed; 'fuck' never destroyed anyone's life.

JEVON: I quite agree. We seem to spend half our lives here trying to find ways of getting round these things. It's tedious in the extreme.

(*This stops* GRANT *for a second*.)

But you're not helping by getting so worked up . . .

GRANT: Oh yes, that's typical of this place. Calm down! Don't get excited! That why all we ever produce is lukewarm piss. Just look at you! In your John Collier slacks! You're scared shitless in case anyone makes a programme that touches a nerve and makes people sit up and be affected. Turn suffering into memorable documentaries so we don't feel so bad about it. Let the odd controversial thing through now and again, but apart from that – keep the trance pills rolling, chaps! You want some real pain? Something truthful? (*Gets videotape out of machine*.) Well, here it is! My God, they'd have to exocet the building to make you look up from your wall-charts and your coloured drawing pins.

LORNA: Grant, if I'm the reason you're feeling upset . . .

GRANT: Don't come the compassionate, Lorna! It doesn't suit you. Sticking icicles into people is more your style. You raise my hopes, then as soon as your precious little promotion's at risk, me and my six years of waiting are dropped like a ton of hot shit. Wheel on David pocket-handkerchief Miles to turn in a shaved corpse of a production and save the day.

LORNA: Now listen, Grant! That show in your hands was threatening to go completely haywire . . .

JEVON: No, no, Lorna. Grant was doing . . . No, no. That was fine. That was fine. I think Grant's got some extremely valid points about the way we make programmes here. Actually. I think at some stage . . . listening to him . . . I think at some stage we should all put our heads together and thrash a few of these things out. It's always good to get grievances out into the open. And I'm sorry, Grant, there's been a sudden change of bowler, but you'll be doing a project of your own in the future, as I'm sure Lorna's told you. So that'll be something for us all to look forward to. However . . .

GRANT: Here we go . . .

JEVON: No, but I think at the moment, quite understandably, you've run up a busy head of steam, and it might be best if you took a week or two's leave. Paid, of course. Come back when the nun show's finished shooting and we'll all sit down together and have a deeper sort of chinwag.

GRANT: You think I'll come back to this shithouse?

JEVON: I think you should take a breather for the moment, Grant. It stinks to high heaven here occasionally, I agree. All the more reason to have periods away and take in some fresh air.

GRANT: (*To* JEVON) The diplomat. You wouldn't recognize a moment of passion if it ran a million volts up your arse.

JEVON: Couple of weeks, Grant. Come in then and we'll talk.
(GRANT *looks at* JEVON *and* LORNA *with impotent bile.*)

GRANT: Cunts!
(*Exit* GRANT.)

JEVON: Ah! (*Smiles reassuringly at* CAROLINE.) Stimulating little tête-à-tête. I think we'll take this (*takes videotape*) for starters. Wouldn't want it gracing the screens of BAFTA

70

tomorrow afternoon, would we? Caroline, pop down to the cutting room and find the genuine article, would you?

CAROLINE: Sure.

(*Exit* CAROLINE.)

JEVON: What do you do to them, Lorna?

LORNA: I don't do anything.

JEVON: If a word of this gets out . . . What was that tape he was showing?

LORNA: I was thinking of using Anne on the nun show.

JEVON: I don't know how that woman ever slipped through the net – the religious skeletons she had in her cupboard.

LORNA: I was looking for something different . . . Something original.

JEVON: I knew it would go wrong, but not this wrong. At least Caroline hasn't gone yet.

LORNA: Stop being melodramatic!

JEVON: There's no melodrama. I gave her a reference just after New Year.

(*This is news to* LORNA.)

Anyway, I'm not concerned with Caroline. She's infantry. It's Grant I'm worried about. If *Private Eye* get hold of all this . . . He's bitter, he's a failure – they thrive on stories by people like him. And with Alexis Colby breathing down his neck at home . . . Situation's tinder dry.

(*Enter* CAROLINE *with tape.*)

CAROLINE: (*Gives it to* JEVON.) This is a copy of the one we sent to BAFTA. It looks all right.

JEVON: Go across and check it. Take a cab.

CAROLINE: (*Going*) OK.

JEVON: Er, Caroline! Have you got a starting date yet?

(CAROLINE *looks embarrassed.*)

It's all right. Lorna knows. You'll understand we need to be able to plan the next month quite carefully in view of what's happened.

CAROLINE: I go in March. I wouldn't have left without . . .

JEVON: No, no, of course not.

LORNA: Where are you going?

71

CAROLINE: I'm going to work for a film company. (*Beat.*) Artificial Eye.

LORNA: Doing what?

CAROLINE: It's not a very big one, but . . . Lots of dogsbody work, I expect. Only they're looking for someone with initiative and how I get on'll depend on what I come up with.

LORNA: But how did you get it?

CAROLINE: Friend who works there. It's a drop in salary and I'll be on three months' probation but I think it's worth the risk.

LORNA: Why didn't you tell me?

CAROLINE: (*Beat.*) I was frightened of what you might do.

LORNA: But, love! You are real television material. I've written reports on you saying as much.

CAROLINE: I'm not sure I want to stay in telly any more.

LORNA: Why on earth not?

(CAROLINE *doesn't have an answer. Pause, as she nervously evades* LORNA's *questioning stare.*)

JEVON: I was saying, by the way, Caroline, to that chap when he rang me . . .

CAROLINE: Maurice.

JEVON: What a discreet child you are. I'm sure you wouldn't want to do anything to gainsay that impression . . .

CAROLINE: Of course not.

JEVON: I don't need to explain how sensitive all this could be . . . Hmm?

(CAROLINE *smiles, and* JEVON *smiles back.*)

So, yes . . . If you could just pop along to BAFTA and check that cassette . . . That'll do nicely.

(LORNA *and* CAROLINE *look at each other briefly. Exit* CAROLINE. LORNA *looks defeated.*)

Getting programmes out on time is your strong point, Lorna. Not cultivating friendships. You should stick to what you're good at.

LORNA: That's what you'd like, isn't it? Stick to being the person you can manage. With you as my only outside activity.

JEVON: Don't let's get into all that again.

LORNA: You just couldn't bear to see me managing on my own.

JEVON: It's the programmes I'm concerned about. I've no hold over your personal life and I don't want to have . . .

LORNA: Precisely!

JEVON: I didn't mean it like that!

LORNA: Five years we've been lovers. And how much of your life does it account for? A tenth? A thirtieth? It's been the whole of mine.

JEVON: You've got your work.

LORNA: Hoh! To keep me occupied! Look at it, Jevon! (*Waves arm round room.*) 'Shaved corpses' Grant called my programmes . . .

JEVON: Lorna, there's a time and a place . . .

LORNA: Do you ever think how I feel, knowing most of my staff detest me? I see myself doing it but I can't stop. And the one time I did; the one time I started to get close to someone, you took it away.

JEVON: You encouraged her to leave. Call her back if she means that much to you.

LORNA: It's right to let people go.

JEVON: Well, stop blathering on about it . . .

LORNA: (*Shouting*) Why am I always alone?
(*Pause, as* JEVON *takes stock.*)

JEVON: Whatever happens in the future, the fact remains we have an immediate problem on our hands. Your entire department has just fallen to pieces and Lyall is going to want to know why. And if the press do get hold of it . . .

LORNA: I'm tired. I'm tired of having to do it all on my own.
(*She starts to sob briefly.*)

JEVON: (*Comforting her*) I know. I know. But we've got to sort this one out or we're in deep water.

LORNA: 'We'?

JEVON: Us, yes. The old firm. We can do it, Lorna. It's how couples get closer, going through bad times together. We've done it before.

LORNA: (*Pause.*) What are we going to do?

JEVON: Well, let's think. Grant goes home not knowing whether

to put the flag out or mess his pants. After doing a bit of
both he realizes the first thing he's got to decide is whether
or not to tell Diana. Panic. Quickly realizes full
implications of what he's done and decides to keep quiet
about it. Goes through three weeks of hate, regret and self-
loathing, at some time during which I drop him a friendly
card inviting him back in for a glass of sherry. I don't
remind him of his behaviour; he's so grateful he backs
down on some of his more ludicrous artistic positions –
tacitly of course. He duly comes back into the fold, does a
programme later on this year . . . We all forget about it.

LORNA: But what if he leaves? What if he does go and tell
everyone?

(*They look apprehensively at each other.*)

SCENE 14

Four months later. Late May. Morning. LORNA *and* GRANT *are
reading the daily newspapers.*

LORNA: *Telegraph*'s reasonable. And that was a good one for
the *Guardian*. One and a half out of five.

GRANT: Not bad.

LORNA: See what the *Standard* has to say later. You've got to
make a *Cathy Come Home* or something like that series
about the Police for them *all* to be ecstatic. I think we've
done quite well.

(*The phone rings.*)

Where's Lizzie got to? (*Picks phone up.*) Social Features?
Melda! Hi! Oh, thank you! Yes, we're just looking at them.
Isn't she a wonderful woman? I know. Even the crew
thought she was fabulous. I think that new wave
treatment's rather effective, don't you? Long silences.
Specially for nuns, yes. Gives it a contemplative effect.
Saves money on the voice-overs too, I can tell you! Oh, the
sunset on the altar. We cheated that slightly, I'm afraid.
Well exactly! SBWN after all. How are you, anyway?
Melda, we must have that lunch some time. I know, but

74

let's make an effort, shall we? Be in touch. Bye, Melda! Blessings! (*Puts phone down.*) Melda singing our praises. Must want something.

GRANT: What's SBWN?

LORNA: Silly buggers won't notice. You not heard that before?

GRANT: No.

LORNA: (*Taking two of the newspapers*) I'll get these run off.

GRANT: Did you talk to Jevon?

LORNA: Yes. He rather agrees with me about your prisoners idea. It's interesting but it smacks a little bit of disabled, one-parent bus shelters somehow. Do you know what I mean?

GRANT: Bit trendy?

LORNA: Not what we're looking for to launch the longer slots.

GRANT: I can still do the aerobics show though?

LORNA: I'd have thought so. Autumn will be a good time for you to start. You've done most of the research, haven't you?

GRANT: Yeah.

LORNA: Well, make sure the pre-production goes smoothly . . . I won't be long.

(*Exit* LORNA.)

GRANT: (*Reads from newspaper:*) 'No sooner did we start to glimpse what really makes a nun tick than we were jolted away into a jumbled collage of stereotyped convent pictures.'

(*He shakes his head and smiles ruefully. Enter* ANNE, *attractively dressed and looking confident.*)

ANNE: Hello!

GRANT: Anne! Hi! I thought you were in Paris?

ANNE: Next week.

GRANT: How's it going?

ANNE: OK. I saw *Habit of a Lifetime* last night.

GRANT: You must have cringed.

ANNE: (*Smiles.*) It was fine.

GRANT: It was bloody awful.

ANNE: Why didn't you direct it?

GRANT: (*Nods in direction of Lorna's desk.*) Why do you think?

ANNE: Everything seemed to be going so well when I left.

GRANT: The sudden spring hit a late frost, I'm afraid.

ANNE: Why?

GRANT: Worried about promotion, pressure from Jevon . . .

ANNE: Yes. I heard she'd gone back to him. (*Beat.*) So what are you doing?

GRANT: Same as before. (*Beat.*) They keep promising me directing slots, but . . . I don't know. Give it till Christmas. I'm going if they haven't given me anything by then. You're well out of it, Anne. Nothing changes. (*Beat.*) But how's life for you?

ANNE: It's OK.

GRANT: Yeah?

ANNE: It's very different working in a big team. There's a lot of travelling, which is nice . . .

(*Enter* LORNA.)

Hello, Lorna!

LORNA: (*Unpleasantly surprised*) Anne!

ANNE: How are you?

LORNA: This is a surprise.

ANNE: I saw the show. I thought I'd pop in.

LORNA: Oh, yes. What did you think?

ANNE: I thought it was fine.

LORNA: We did our best. Perhaps not quite what you had in mind, but . . .

ANNE: No, no . . .

LORNA: One or two contingencies had to be made. How's the Renaissance?

ANNE: Impressionism at the moment. Yes, it's going well. I'm just about to leave for Paris.

LORNA: (*Attending to her work*) Autumn shooting?

ANNE: Autumn, yes. September, October.

LORNA: And how's Gavin?

ANNE: He's quite nice.

LORNA: Forty-one sixty-four by three is one two four ninety-two . . . Why've they given me an extra five seventy-five?

ANNE: Expenses?

LORNA: What? Oh, yes.

ANNE: How are you?

LORNA: We're fine. We're fine. Don't tell me they've actually coughed up for that carafe of wine. I don't believe it. They have. Yes, we're preparing the tracks for something Grant can cut his teeth on. Longer slots coming up in the New Year too, so . . .

ANNE: Oh, you got them!

LORNA: Finally.

ANNE: Well done!

GRANT: How's Gavin tackling the show?

ANNE: Lots of Peter Sengora walking round art galleries talking into camera.

LORNA: The art critic?

ANNE: It's a bit predictable.

GRANT: Good opportunity though.

ANNE: Oh, yes, but . . . Working here was more exciting in a way. (*Beat.*) Do you remember that time at the abbey, Lorna?

LORNA: Doing the research, yes. She should have been with us in the magistrates' court, shouldn't she, Grant?

GRANT: The lies people try to get away with.

ANNE: It was a good time though, wasn't it, that weekend?

LORNA: At the convent? Yes, it was fun. Here are those production stills we were looking for, Grant.

GRANT: Oh, yes.

LORNA: Lizzie must have put them in the wrong file.

ANNE: I got your message that time. I tried ringing back but you were never around.

LORNA: I've been terribly busy, Anne.

(LORNA *picks up the phone and dials, giving* ANNE *a brief, patronizing smile.*)

ANNE: Oh, I'm sure. I was just passing, so . . .

(*Awkward pause.*)

Well, I can see you're both busy . . .

LORNA: Why the hell don't they answer?

ANNE: My meeting's at eleven . . . I'll be off.

GRANT: Keep in touch.

ANNE: Yes. (*To* LORNA) Perhaps we could have a drink some time?

LORNA: That'd be . . . (*Into phone*) Oh, could I speak to Philip
Holland please? OK. Could you tell him Lorna Brooks
phoned? Just in case I don't reach him. Thanks. Bye. (*Puts
phone down.*) Sorry, Anne. Yes. A drink. That would be
very nice. When are you back?

ANNE: Couple of weeks.

LORNA: Give me a ring. That would be lovely.

ANNE: Talk about the old times.

LORNA: Nothing like the past.

ANNE: No, well . . .

LORNA: Lovely to see you again, Anne.

ANNE: Yes. And you. I'll . . . Bye.

GRANT: Bye, Anne!

LORNA: God bless!
  (*Exit* ANNE.)
  Rave from the grave.

GRANT: She looked well.

LORNA: (*Picks up phone.*) See if I can get him at home.

GRANT: Who are you chasing?

LORNA: Philip Holland? You remember – that interesting chap I
met at that directors' weekend. Just starting out. Did that
old-age thing for Linsy Eldon that I had to turn down.

GRANT: Oh, yes. It was really good.

LORNA: He's in big demand now. I want him to guest direct
something for us if he's free.

GRANT: (*Going*) I must go see how my availabilities are going for
the autumn.

LORNA: Grant!
  (*Pause, as* LORNA *lets the phone ring a little longer before
  putting it down.*)
  You'll keep things tight on the pre-production, won't you?
  (*Beat.*) You're within an ace of full-time directing. A
  smooth run-up on the aerobics show . . .

GRANT: (*Pause.*) Sure. (*Beat.*) Sure.
  (*Brief pause, then* LORNA *smiles faintly by way of letting him
  go. Exit* GRANT. LORNA *smiles to herself, then feeling herself
  alone in the office, a flicker of deep anxiety crosses her face.
  The phone rings and she answers it.*)

LORNA: (*Into phone*) Social Features? Ah, Jevon. I checked, yes. There's a six thirty-five from Victoria that shouldn't be too crowded if we want to go on Friday. Gets into Hastings at quarter to eight. Mm. I was just about to pop along to *you*, actually. Shall I. . . ? No, darling, it's no problem. No problem.

(*She puts the phone down.*)

I've got plenty of time . . .